Somet

The C #10

Bre raemer

Something to Lose

The Cedarville Series

Bree Kraemer

Published by Bree Kraemer, 2019.

Something to Lose

First edition. April 3, 2019.

Written by Bree Kraemer.

Also by Bree Kraemer

The Only Series

Only By His Touch
Only With Trust
If Only
Only You
Only For Love

Cedarville Novels

An Unexpected Home
Capturing Us
Choosing You
Better Together
A Chance Worth Taking
Forever Starts Here (Novella)
After All These Years
Won't Let You Down
Say When
Something To Lose
Finally Home

Friends & Brothers

Sky High Love
Bridge To Love
When It's Love

Rockstar Romance

The Right Note (Big City Heat Anthology)
Pick Me

Christmas Novella

Light Me Up

The Beckmeyer Family

Chapter 1

It was after one in the morning and instead of sleeping in his bed, Wyatt was up roaming the halls of his apartment building.

His.

It was all his.

Well technically it also belonged to his brother, Flynn but it only involved him a little. Wyatt was in charge. Hence the walking around at one in the morning.

He loved walking the halls in the middle of the night just taking in what belonged to him. He'd never owned anything until he'd moved to Cedarville. Not a car, not a house, not a pet. Nothing.

But things were changing.

A year ago he'd been so burnt out after only four years as a stockbroker that he'd been having daily panic attacks. They'd gotten so bad that there would be days he could barely get out of bed. His mom, dad and brother had all pleaded with him to make a change.

So he did.

He moved to Cedarville.

There had been no way that he was moving back to where his mom and dad lived in Indiana. He loved them, probably more than most twenty-six year olds loved their parents, but that didn't mean he wanted to live in the same town as them.

He wanted to make it on his own but he also wanted a family.

Flynn was the next best thing.

His brother was his hero in all ways that mattered. While his parents had saved him by adopting him, Flynn had saved him by showing him that brother didn't have to mean blood. He'd stayed by his side those first few nights after the adoption, never once making Wyatt feel like a burden. Instead, he'd felt loved for possibly the first time in his life.

And it never stopped. Flynn had always been there for him, no matter what. He'd been there at fifteen when he'd been sure his heart was breaking thanks to his best friend dating the girl he'd liked and then again when he'd wrecked his mom's car when he wasn't even supposed to be driving it. And when he'd decided to move to New York City for college, Flynn visited all the time so that feeling homesick was never even an option.

It was an easy decision for him that after his breakdown, the only place he wanted to live was where Flynn lived.

Cedarville.

The town was as amazing as Flynn had always said, making Wyatt sad that he'd never once in almost ten years visited him there.

While Flynn was the epitome of what a brother should be, Wyatt was barely holding his head above water.

He was one of those people who if you texted him, he might text you back...three days later.

The life of a stockbroker had been fast paced and high stress. So answering calls that weren't immediately important wasn't a high priority.

Not anymore though. He'd promised both himself and Flynn that things would be different now that he was in Cedarville. He would be present in life and enjoy his family and friends more.

Not that he had any real knowledge of how friendship worked. In New York, it was dog eat dog and people only pretended to be your friend to get what they wanted. But in Cedarville, it was different. Everyone was so nice. Nice enough that they'd been including him for months in their gatherings or parties just because he was Flynn's brother.

His soon to be sister-in-law, Joy, might also have something to do with that. She could be demanding and forceful when she wanted to be, making it hard for people to say no to her.

He laughed out loud as he turned the corner, his hand smoothing over the fresh coat of paint he'd just put on the day before. His brother was getting married to a woman who, let's face it, had him by his balls. Flynn didn't care though. He saw nothing but stars when it came to Joy and after spending more and more time with her, Wyatt could see why.

She was his perfect match.

As he approached the front, he scanned the hallway to make sure everything was in place. After Joy had moved out of the ground floor apartment, he'd moved in. When he'd first purchased the building there had been no vacancies, so he'd had to rent elsewhere. Of course Flynn had offered to let him stay at his place, but he didn't want to be any more of a burden than he already was. But as soon as Joy moved out, he'd moved in. He enjoyed being on hand in case a tenant needed him. It made him feel useful for maybe the first time ever.

Being a stockbroker had been effortless for him. Numbers and money came easy to him, almost like breathing. Which was why at twenty-six, he could leave behind a job, move towns, and buy a building.

Two actually.

He'd made himself enough money to be comfortable but at the same time made himself sick. No more. Now he was living the small town life where he hoped he made a difference to the people who lived in his building.

He entered his apartment, making sure to quietly shut the door behind him. He didn't want to wake anyone up with a slamming door.

After years of living on four hours of sleep a night, his body still hadn't adjusted to getting more. He'd finally settled on a routine of going to bed late rather than getting up at three or four and being wide awake. Midnight was his new bedtime but tonight he'd been restless and unable to fall asleep. So he walked and walked and walked and now he was finally ready to hit the hay.

Settling into his bed, he made sure his phone was still on just in case anyone needed to get ahold of him, flipped off his light and finally closed his eyes,

He was asleep in seconds.

After two hours of paperwork and paying bills, he was on his way into downtown Cedarville. If you could call it that. Cedarville was not a big town and the downtown was basically a town square of sorts. There were about two blocks of buildings strung along both sides of Main Street with a few more in either direction. Plus a cute park and a small fountain. Your basic small town staples.

It was also home to his second building which he so happened to rent out to Joy. She had opened a nail salon less than a month ago in the small retail space. It had felt weird at first, charging her for the space, but she had argued that this was business and that as much as he needed it to feel useful, she needed it more.

She was an independent woman who didn't take handouts.

Which was hard on Flynn because if he'd had it his way, he'd have purchased the building himself.

He'd seen her point though and rented it at a reasonable price that suited them both.

Finding a parking spot, he shut off his car and stepped out. There was a chill in the air but otherwise it was an unseasonably warm day for November. He found Flynn standing on the sidewalk, right in front of Joy's salon.

"Don't you have anything better to do than hang out here all day?" He slammed the car door shut and stepped up onto the sidewalk.

Flynn rolled his eyes. "There is nothing better than hanging out with Joy all day but that's not why I'm here."

Concerned, he asked, "Is everything okay? Mom? Dad?"

He lifted a hand. "Everything is fine with them."

Wyatt punched his arm. “Don’t scare me like that.”

“Sorry.” He shrugged, not at all fazed by the punch. “I actually wanted to talk to you about my wedding?”

“Did you guys set a date?” He knew Joy wanted simple but he also knew that Flynn wanted her to have a dream wedding.

“We have. New Years’ Eve.”

He blinked in surprise. “That’s soon.”

“It is but we both decided it would be fun to throw a huge party where everyone got to dress up and be fancy to start the new year.”

“Pretty smart idea. What do you need from me?”

“I’m hoping that you’ll be my best man.”

“Really?” He was shocked.

“You’re my brother, Wyatt. Who else would I ask?”

“I don’t know. I guess I never really thought about it.”

“I want you beside me as I marry the woman I love. Please say you’ll do it?”

He smiled. “I will absolutely do it.”

He nodded. “Great.” He stood oddly for a second before giving him a brotherly hug. “I’m not sure I’ve told you this, but I’m really glad you moved here.” He stepped back. “Family was the one thing missing from this place.”

“Thanks.” He looked around. “I really love it here. Felt like home almost from the beginning.”

“Was the same for me.”

“You wanna come with me to check out the building?”

“Nah. If I go in there, I won’t want to leave. Tell Joy I’ll see her at home.”

Laughing, he slapped him on the back as he walked past him. “You’re so whipped.”

“You bet your ass I am!”

Wyatt was still on a high from Flynn asking him to be his best man when he walked inside the building. He didn't see Joy and assumed she was in the back.

"Joy, you here?" he shouted out.

"Be right out!" he heard from the back.

While he waited he began to walk around and take in the place. It had only been open a month and the work that Flynn and Joy had done to make it a nail salon was amazing. When he'd purchased it, it was just an empty rectangular space. Now it housed six nail stations on one side and six pedicure stations on the other side. There were mirrors on the walls and several sinks in the back. Joy had somehow taken a small space and made it homey and comfortable. As far as he knew, the place was always busy. So busy that Joy was already thinking about hiring another tech.

"Hey," she said as she emerged from the back room. "Sorry to keep you waiting."

"You aren't. I just wanted to come by and check on the place. Make sure everything is working right and that there are no problems."

"You don't have to do that, you know. Flynn will take care of anything I need."

He shrugged. "I know but it's my building and I don't want you to feel like I am shirking my responsibilities."

"Wyatt, I love you but don't be an ass. No one would ever feel like you are shirking responsibility."

"I just want to do this right."

"I know because I feel the same way about this place. But we are family or at least we will be soon and I need you as a brother more than I need you as a landlord. Your brother keeps me on my toes and since you know him best, you need to be here for me."

Wyatt shook his head, unable to stop the laughter from bubbling out. "Somehow I think you are the one who keeps him on his toes. But I agree, let's be family first."

She stuck out her hand for him to shake. "Deal. Now tell me, did the love of my life ask you anything a little while ago?"

"Maybe, I wasn't really paying attention," he joked. "Something about New Year's Eve and standing next to him."

She punched his shoulder. "You are such a smartass."

More seriously, he said, "I would love nothing more than to stand up with him at your wedding."

"Good. He was nervous to ask you. As if you'd dare say no." She pushed her hip out, her hand resting on it.

"He's done so much for me over the years that I would never say no to anything he asked. But this...being his best man. That is my total pleasure."

"Brace yourself, cause you are about to get something that very few people get from me."

He eyed her carefully. "I'm not sure Flynn would approve."

She smiled and then surprised him by wrapping her arms around his back in a hug. "I'm so happy Flynn has you and that now, I have you."

He relaxed, hugging her back. "Flynn is a lucky guy."

"Oh I know," she said as she let him go and stood back. "I tell him everyday."

"I'm just gonna take a look in the back and make sure everything looks good and then I'll get out of your hair."

She pointed her arm in the direction of the back. "Be my guest."

He quickly and efficiently looked over the back including the bathroom to make sure everything worked correctly. He wasn't a contractor like Flynn but over the last year, he'd learned enough to become fairly proficient, at least at spotting problems. When he was satisfied, he went back out front and found Joy.

"Oh before you leave, can you do me a favor?"

"Sure."

She walked to the front counter, reaching for something on the bottom shelf. "Can you deliver this to Norah? She asked if I'd order it for her and I just don't have time to run it over to her today."

She was holding a couple of bottles of what looked like lotion. "Norah who lives across the hall from me?"

"Yeah." She looked at him strangely. "You have met her right?"

"I actually haven't."

"Wyatt, you own the building. How is it that you haven't met her?"

"She never has any problems or concerns, her rent checks are always on time and she causes no issues. There was no need."

She rolled her eyes, dropping her head backward. "That's the stupidest thing I've ever heard. She rents an apartment in a building you own, you should have met her by now." She put both bottles into a brown paper bag.

He reached out, snatching the bag from her hands. "So I'll meet her when I drop these off."

"Whatever, I have too much to do to spend any of it babysitting you. I'll text her to let her know you'll be dropping them off. Oh and be nice to her. She's shy."

"Everyone is shy compared to you."

"I can't argue with that but Norah is actually shy. So tread carefully."

"Okay, crazy." He lifted his arm to wave as he walked out the door.

As he made his way to his truck, he tried to remember if he'd ever even seen the elusive Norah Baker. He wasn't sure he had. There was one time a couple weeks ago that he'd walked out of his apartment and she'd been going into hers across the hall. He'd seen the back of her, her blonde hair laying across her back. But by the time he'd said hello, she'd already shut her door.

As far as he could remember that was the only time he'd seen her.

Now that he thought about it, she was the only tenant he hadn't met yet. But did it really matter? Like he'd told Joy, she paid on time, was never late, never caused problems and didn't ask him for anything.

Why did it matter that he hadn't technically met her?

For some reason though it was nagging at him and he couldn't stop thinking that it made him a bad person for not even trying to meet and connect with her.

That was going to change today. In just a few minutes he would knock on the door of the mystery tenant and finally after six months meet her.

Chapter 2

Day four hundred and thirty-two was the day that was finally about to make her crack.

Four hundred and thirty-two days since she'd run away from her former life, leaving everything behind.

Four hundred and thirty-two days since she'd had a real conversation with anyone.

Sighing, she paced her small apartment. She'd rented it because it was small but now after four hundred and thirty-two days of being mostly confined to it, she was regretting the choice.

She was starting to feel claustrophobic. Summer had been a little better because she could go out onto her patio to sit and take in the fresh air. But now that it was getting cooler, she had less and less of those days.

She missed her life. Well part of her life. The part where she had friends and family and a job.

A purpose.

She did not miss her controlling, emotionally abusive fiance. The man who was the reason she was stuck inside her small apartment.

When she'd met Brett she'd been Norah Evers, only daughter of Steven and Pam Evers. Her father had started a software company, Eversware, that blew up in the early nineties and had stayed that way her whole life. She'd grown up being the only heir to his massive fortune. But like her dad and mom, she didn't care as much about the money as she did about being a good person. After college, where she double majored in computer science and finance, because she'd wanted to be able to work in her dad's company but also wanted to know enough about money to help people, she took on the role of charity donations.

And she did help people.

Eversware donated more than half its profits to charities that helped make sure people could live the life they wanted.

Then three years ago, she'd met Brett Dalton. He'd been hired as the VP of Infrastructure and almost immediately they'd started dating. He'd started off sweet, attentive and loving. And he'd stayed that way until her parents had both died in a car crash.

When she'd needed him as her rock, he'd instead turned into a controlling bastard who day in and day out mentally abused her. He told her what to do. Didn't like her philanthropy and hated that she had anything to do with the company.

She soon found out that he wanted Eversware for himself.

His plan was to marry her, take over and change everything.

She wasn't about to let that happen.

So she'd secured the business, making sure that he couldn't touch it and planned to leave him. Only he didn't take it well. He was furious and during their argument went berserk, calling her names and then actually hitting her.

She was dumbfounded that the man she thought she'd loved could do such a thing. And she had no one. Her parents were gone, there was no other family to turn to. But what he'd said after he struck her was what had put her in the position she was in now. He'd said that he'd kill her like he'd done with her parents.

She had no idea if it was true, but she'd gone to the police just the same. But they didn't believe her. Worse, they believed and liked him. He'd laughed in her face after he'd been questioned by the police saying no one would ever believe her. He'd gripped her arm so hard that she'd had bruises for days. Not knowing what to do, she'd panicked. The next day, she liquidated as much money as she could, dyed her dark brown hair blonde, purchased a new identity and left California for the midwest. She needed to get lost and figured there was no better place to do that than the middle of nowhere.

She'd kept her first name the same because it was her grandma's and she just couldn't change it and still feel like the same person. But she'd changed her last name to Baker. Plain and unforgettable. When looking for towns to live in, she'd spotted the small town of Cedarville thanks to the lake.

Dragonfly Lake.

Dragonflies had been something of an obsession of hers as a young girl. As a family, they'd once visited a lake in southern Canada and the whole week they'd been there, she'd been fascinated by the dragonflies.

As soon as she'd spotted the lake, she'd known that was where she had to go.

Plus, Brett had no idea about that memory so it wasn't something he could use to find her.

She'd known it was drastic but she was weak and afraid. Scared for her own life and sad at the loss of her parents.

This was the only decision she could think of to get away from the fear.

So for four hundred and thirty-two days she'd hidden away in the small town of Cedarville, only leaving her apartment once or twice a week.

She was miserable, sad, lonely and worst of all, still scared.

She'd seen Brett on television several times or read articles about him, each time begging the public to help find her. His devoted fiance had gone missing and he was so distraught.

Made her want to puke.

But also made her glad she'd listened to her instincts and ran. He was a monster and if she'd stayed she'd be either stuck in an abusive relationship or dead.

Probably the last one.

Tears she hadn't known were there, fell down her cheeks. She missed her mom and dad tremendously. Missed her dad's smile and the way her mom would roll her eyes at his corny jokes. They'd been such amazing people and their deaths had shattered her heart into a million little pieces.

When she'd run, she'd left her phone, computer and all trackable electronics behind. So the only picture she had of them was the one she'd grabbed quickly when she'd thrown a bag together.

One picture to remind her of the life she used to have, one she so desperately missed.

Swiping her hands under her eyes, she wiped away the tears.

No, she wasn't going to do this. She wasn't going to dwell on the past. She was alive, had plenty of money thanks to her parents, and a roof over her head. It was more than a lot of people had.

She'd even made a friend...sort of. Joy used to live across the hall and even though she'd tried to keep her at arm's length, Joy had pushed her way into her life. She would stop by once every couple of weeks and generously give her a manicure and pedicure and some human interaction, which was far more important. Joy had never asked for an explanation on why she didn't leave her apartment and Norah hadn't volunteered the info. She assumed Joy thought she was one of those people who feared the outside world.

Their friendship would seem odd to anyone on the outside but to Norah, it was her only saving grace.

Her phone dinged and she leaned down to grab it from the second hand coffee table she'd bought at a yard sale when she'd first moved to town.

Joy:

I'm not going to be able to stop by today but I got in those lotions you talked about. Wyatt is going to drop them off.

Fear crept up her spine. Wyatt was the landlord. She'd never met him nor had she talked to him. He'd only purchased the building six months ago and there had never been any reason to have communication with him.

She had however seen him.

Through her peephole.

When she'd snoop on him going in and out of his apartment.

When it had still been warm out, he'd go for runs early in the morning shirtless.

His bare chest was a work of art. A work of art that she wanted to bite.

Groaning, she fell onto the couch. She had never been an overtly sexual person. She'd liked sex just fine but really it had never been anything to write home about. Her first time had been when she was seventeen with her high school boyfriend, Aaron. He was sweet and they'd been going out for six months. But more, she didn't want to go to college as a virgin. So she'd given in and they'd had sex.

Was blah a feeling? Because that's what it had been.

All four times they'd done it.

Then in college she'd had what she considered the obligatory one night stand after a party her freshman year. It was slightly better than blah but only by a fraction. The alcohol probably gave it that extra oomph.

She'd finally given her first bow job the summer between freshman and sophomore year and surprisingly while she didn't love the guy, she loved the feeling of having a hard cock in her mouth and under her control. She could almost orgasm from that alone.

Although she never had.

After that, sex was a little more fun but the actual penetration still wasn't her favorite. She did it because it's what you did when you had a boyfriend and were in a relationship.

Then came Brett.

He never wanted her to go down on him which made each time less fun for her. And the sex, well, he liked it a certain way and wouldn't vere off track.

He'd only do missionary or doggy.

Nothing else.

And he held her down hard during both of those.

Looking back she understood that it was his way of keeping control. She should have known and not settled.

She never would again.

If she ever had the chance to have sex again, she was going to make sure it was what she wanted. How she liked it. None of this my way and you just have to deal crap.

That was a big if though. She rarely left her apartment so the chances of finding someone to have sex with her was slim to none.

A vision of Wyatt flashed in her head.

His dark, almost black hair that was long around his neck and ears. His seemingly always tan skin even though it was November. His biteable chest that glistened with sweat after a run.

He was sex personified.

Which was one of the reasons she'd kept her distance. She didn't need to get involved with anyone who would question anything about her.

But that didn't stop her from thinking about him.

All. The. Time.

Sometimes she wondered if she'd think about anyone that she saw since she was locked up in her apartment. But then she'd remember that she had gone into town and seen some good looking guys and not once did she picture them in her head while pleasuring herself.

Only Wyatt.

She looked down at herself, taking in her sweats, t-shirt and heavy socks. This was the perfect outfit to open the door in when he came by. There was nothing sexy or provocative about it meaning there was no way he could look at her and do anything but hand her the lotion and leave.

She wanted to blend in, making sure he didn't give her another thought.

Norah:

No problem. I appreciate you getting them for me.

She took a deep breath, hoping to slow her heartbeat. She wasn't sure when he'd be stopping by but she figured it would be the next time he came home. That could be anytime at all.

Wanting to keep herself occupied, she reached for her laptop to do some work.

While she didn't need the money, she liked to stay busy or else she'd go crazy. After about a month of being alone in the apartment, she'd started writing. Nothing she ever thought she'd show to anyone but stories about young girls who are coming of age in the world. After six months, she'd had three full books written and now after over a year, she had eight.

Someday she might publish them, but for now, they were her savior.

A loud knock on the door startled her, immediately thinking the worst. But then she remembered it was probably Wyatt. Setting her laptop aside, she steadied her breathing, walked to the door and checked the peephole.

Where she found Wyatt.

She told herself to relax as she turned the knob and opened the door.

"Hi, Miss Baker, I'm Wyatt Murray the landlord."

She swallowed before saying, "Hi."

"Joy asked me to drop these off to you." He held out a brown paper bag.

"Thank you." She reached for it, her fingers brushing his as she took it from him. She felt a weird electricity as their fingers touched, her whole body going on alert. Inside she was a mess but she kept her composure on the outside.

"I also wanted to introduce myself to you since we hadn't met yet."

She stepped back, planning to close the door. She needed to put space between them. "It's nice to meet you."

He stopped the door with his hand before it was fully closed. "If you ever need anything please let me know."

She nodded and pushed harder, finally able to close the door. Covering her mouth with her hand, she slid to the floor right where she was.

What the hell was that?

Her fingers still tingled from his slight touch and her heart was pounding inside her chest. She felt as if she'd been struck by lightning. Her whole body was on alert.

She listened closely, hearing his footfalls and then his door latch closed.

Finally she let out the breath she'd been holding, leaning back against the door. She'd never in her whole life had a reaction like the one she'd just had. In her line of work, she'd come across good looking guys all the time. She'd been able to carry on conversations and work closely with them. Nothing like what had just happened had ever happened before.

She wished she could just chalk it up to lack of male companionship for a year but she didn't think it was that. There was something about him. Something different that her body was aware of without her even knowing him.

Closing her eyes, she did what she always did when she needed answers. She called up an image of her mom. In life, her mom had always been there if she'd needed to talk about anything. And that hadn't changed. She knew it was stupid and probably made her crazy, but she had no one else.

And for twenty minutes she sat, leaning against the door, asking her mom for advice.

Crazy was relative.

Chapter 3

Inside his apartment, Wyatt struggled to figure out what had just happened. Norah Baker was nothing special. At least at first glance. Baggy clothes that hid her figure. Messy, dull, blonde hair pulled into a ponytail. And a face that was bare of make-up, making her look no older than twenty-one.

There should be nothing special about her.

His heart shouldn't be beating so fast that he was afraid he was going to have a heart attack. He shouldn't recall her image in his mind and wonder if her skin was as soft as it looked. And he should in no way want to go back over there just to talk to her.

She'd given him nothing. She'd barely even been friendly.

And yet his mind — and other parts of his body — couldn't stop thinking about her.

With his mind on her, he strode into the room he was using as an office. He wanted to look through her file again. He'd gone through everyone's when he'd first bought the building but he didn't remember anything that stood out about her.

Now he needed to know more.

Finding it in his file cabinet, he sat down at his desk. Inside the file though, there was almost nothing. Her name, a copy of her driver's license, a copy of the cashiers check for first, last and deposit, and a copy of each rent check since.

Nothing else.

Pulling the file of another tenant, he opened it to find the same along with a background check. He pulled another file. Again a background check. He pulled all the rest and all of them had background checks.

Hers was the only one without.

It seemed odd to him that the previous owner would do one for everyone but her. Had he known her personally? That was a possibility but from what he knew, she wasn't a native to Cedarville. That didn't necessarily mean the owner hadn't known her. She could have been a relative or family friend. There could be tons of reasons.

None of that helped Wyatt though. He had no info on her.

Pulling his laptop forward, he powered it on and pulled up the internet. He could at least look her up and see what he could find. Only when he typed her name into the search engine, nothing came up.

Not one thing.

He went to Facebook and searched for her there. Same thing. Nothing.

How did someone make it to her age without a digital footprint? Not only that, but how did she make money? There was no employer listed in her file nor was there a work history.

She was invisible.

Shaking his head, he stood, grabbed the file and walked back through his apartment. He needed more and knew just where to go.

Brandon.

Brandon Graham was the chief of police in Cedarville and if anyone could help him out it would be him.

He drove back into town, parking in front of the police station. He probably should have called to make sure Brandon was even working, but he'd been in such a hurry to find out info on Norah that he'd just gone with his gut.

Luckily Brandon was in his office.

"Wyatt," he stood, coming around his desk shaking his hand, "good to see you."

"Do you have a few minutes?"

"Sure." He closed the door behind them, each of them taking a seat. "What's up?"

"I was going through my tenant files and I came across one that doesn't seem to have a background check. I was wondering if maybe you knew her or knew who she was?" He passed the file across the desk.

Brandon opened it, leaning back as he did so. "I was wondering if you'd question this."

"So you know her?"

"I don't. But when she rented the place from Carl, he came to me. He liked her and really wanted to help her out but since she had no info, he wanted me to check her out."

"And did you?" He'd moved to the end of the chair, literally on the edge of his seat.

"I did." He closed the file, laying it back on his desk. "I'm not sure I'm comfortable telling you what I found."

"Is she dangerous?" That would surprise him.

"No. Not at all."

"Just tell me what you told Carl?"

"I didn't tell Carl anything. He asked if she was legit or if she'd cause trouble. When I told him no, he said that was all he needed to know. We left it at that."

"But you know something about her that you aren't willing to tell me?" What could it possibly be?

"I do but I think before I tell you — or maybe she tells you — I should talk to her."

"Why now?"

"Because now you are looking into her and want to know. It could change things."

"What things?" He was so confused.

Brandon stood. "I need to talk to Norah first."

Wyatt also stood. "I don't understand any of this."

"I know but I promise you, she is not dangerous nor is she involved in anything weird or odd." He walked around his desk. "After I talk with her, I will get back in touch with you."

He left the station unsure of what had just happened. Brandon knew something but wasn't willing to tell him. What could that mean?

Was she a criminal? Had she done something bad? His mind was spinning a million miles a minute.

He needed a distraction.

So he walked next door to Ryan's law office where he found Avery front and center.

"Wyatt, hey how are you?"

"Good. Just out and about and thought I'd stop by."

She eyed him suspiciously. "You are always out and about and yet you never stop by. What gives?"

Avery was Joy's sister and while he'd heard stories about how she used to be shy and quiet, that definitely wasn't the case now. He shrugged. "Just needed to chat."

"To me or to Ryan?"

Good question. "You, I think." The answer surprised himself as much as it did her by the look on her face. He'd been sure that it was Ryan who he'd wanted to talk to.

"Come sit." She directed him to a small couch where she also sat down. "You look a little confused."

"I am." He removed his jacket, laying it across his legs. "Has Joy ever mentioned Norah who lives across the hall from me?"

"Yeah, a few times. Says she's shy and timid but sweet."

"'Until today, I'd never met her."

Her brow furrowed. "How is that possible? She rents an apartment in your building?"

He lifted a hand. "I know, Joy already gave me the third degree. That's not the issue here. After I met her and she was a little odd, I went to double check her file. Only there was virtually nothing in it."

"What is normally in a tenant file?"

"Most of the time it's a background check with a list of previous employers, last known residents and references. Things like that."

"And what did hers have?"

"Just copies of her drivers license and the cashiers check showing she paid first and last month along with the deposit."

She pursed her lips, a finger lifting to tap against them. "That is odd. Did you ask her?"

He shook his head. "She was so withdrawn and unapproachable the first time I knocked on her door that I didn't want to spook her. Instead I went to Brandom. Which was even odder. It seems he knows something about her but he's not willing to tell me."

"Brandon has to have his reasons for doing that, as weird as it seems."

"He said he needed to talk to her first but that he promised she wasn't dangerous or trouble."

"There you go then. You got your answer."

"How is that an answer? I have no info on this woman and she is living right across the hall from me."

"The one thing I've learned about this town, Wyatt, is that sometimes you have to take things as they are. Don't question everything, just enjoy it."

"I was doing that. I thought. But this really threw me for a loop. I came here to live a stress free life and relax. Not to worry that a person I'm renting to is a serial killer."

"She's not a serial killer, dummy. Brandon told you she wasn't dangerous, you need to remember that. He'd never let anything bad happen in this town. He loves it too much."

"I guess you're right." He let out an exhausted breath. His heart was beating fast in his chest, as it had been since the moment Norah Baker had opened her door to him. It felt eerily like when he'd had his panic attacks in New York but at the same time different.

He did not want to go back to the person he'd been there. He liked this version of himself. The version that took each day one at a time and didn't stress over the small things.

"Take it from me, Wyatt, life is too short to worry all the time. Let Brandon do his job and I'm sure everything will work out for the best."

"Thanks, Avery. I appreciate you talking to me."

"Anytime." She stood. "I could really get used to being the person people come to for advice."

"Oh God, if you take that away from Carly, she will throw a fit." Wyatt looked up when he heard Ryan's voice and found him standing just outside his office door. "Unless of course you like to watch girls fighting."

He stood, walking over to shake Ryan's hand. "Can't say I've ever given it much thought but considering that one of the women in question is pregnant, and they are both married, it probably wouldn't be as fun as it sounds."

"What's going on, man?"

"Not much, just came in for a little advice."

"Something I can help you with? Thinking of buying another building?"

"Nah, no money for that." He used Ryan as his lawyer for his new business. "Avery was able to help me out." He hoped.

"Good. I'm always here if you need something. Not to talk and run, but I'm meeting Addison for lunch. And let me tell you, you do not keep an eight month pregnant woman waiting for food."

"I'll walk out with you." He turned toward Avery. "Thanks again."

"Anytime."

He and Ryan walked out, him going to his truck and Ryan walking several doors over to meet up with Addison at the deli. Because owning a couple of buildings didn't take up that much of his time, he had plenty of time to do the things he liked to do.

And any other day, he'd love that. Relish it really. But not today. Today he was wondering what the hell was going on with Brandon and Norah. Would he ever find out anything about her or would he move forward knowing nothing more than he currently knew?

It was frustrating.

And not just because he didn't know anything about her. But because the shot of electricity that coursed through his body at the slight brush of her fingers against his, was something that he'd never felt before in his life.

And fuck if he didn't want to to feel it again.

Soon.

Maybe all the time.

Groaning at the trail his thoughts were taking, he turned on his truck and headed for home.

With the stress of his job the last few years, he'd been without female companionship. Before that though, through college, he'd been somewhat of a manwhore. He hadn't slept with every woman he'd met, but neither did he stop himself if the opportunity presented itself. Sex was fun, or so he'd thought. After a while though, it had just gotten old. Meeting someone, only to have sex and never see them again didn't hold the appeal it had when he was younger.

So he'd thrown himself into his work, leaving himself no time for anything else.

His hand had been his only form of sex in almost two years.

Jesus, he was a loser.

What twenty-six year old went that long without sex?

It wasn't that he hadn't had offers either. In New York and in Cedarville, women came onto him. None of them had appealed to him.

Until that morning and Norah.

Something about her had ignited a flame inside him that had been dormant for too long.

Great, he wanted to have sex with a criminal. Just what he needed to keep the stress out of his life. And yes, he realized he was exaggerating and that she probably wasn't a criminal, but until he knew for sure, he had nothing else to think.

Reaching his apartment, he saw Brandon's cruiser parked in the lot. That meant he was there and talking to Norah.

With his stomach turning round and round, he walked into the building. Before he could enter his apartment though, Brandon came out of Norah's.

"Oh good, you're here."

Turning, he pulled his door shut again. "Yeah, just got back."

"If you wouldn't mind, could you come join Norah and I for a few minutes. She has some things she needs to tell you."

Something in him wanted to run into her apartment, stand in front of her and tell her that it didn't matter. That nothing she said would change how his body already wanted her. How she already made him feel alive without them even knowing each other.

Instead, he re-locked his door and followed Brandon into her apartment. She was sitting on the couch, her legs folded up under her, hands fidgeting in her lap. She looked vulnerable, not at all something he was equipped to deal with.

"Norah, you know Wyatt," Brandon said, taking a seat next to her on the couch.

She nodded but didn't look up at him. He sat down in the chair closest to Brandon figuring that would make her more comfortable.

"Norah has a few things she'd like to tell you about her life before she came to Cedarville." He looked back and forth between Wyatt and Norah. "Whenever you're ready," he said to her.

She visibly swallowed but finally looked up, her eyes catching his. "I'm sorry I lied to you and to everyone but I needed to be invisible and this was the only way I knew how." She looked down at her lap again. "Two years ago my parents died in a car crash. It was the worst day of my life. But I turned to my fiance for support which should have been easy, right?" She let out a choked laugh. "Boy was I wrong. He turned out to only be using me for my money and position in the company my dad had started years before. As soon as my parents were gone, he changed. He became controlling, and mentally abusive." She looked back up, first looking at Brandon then toward him. "The day he physically struck me was the last straw for me. We fought badly and he, in a roundabout way, made it sound like he had something to do with the death of my parents. I was dumbfounded and unsure of what to do. Especially when he told me that if I wasn't careful, I'd end up like them."

"He threatened to kill you?" Wyatt had been silent up until that point but was aghast at what she was insinuating.

"That's what it sounded like to me. So I did what any normal person would do. I went to the police. Only they didn't believe me. Said he was a good guy and would never do something like that. They did question him though but that only made him angrier. That night his rage was out of control and he gripped my arms with a strength that gave me bruises which lasted for days."

She stopped, leaning forward to take a sip of water. Wyatt watched her with newfound admiration. This woman had been through the ringer and here he was making her tell him her story.

He was an ass.

"You don't have to keep going. I think I can see what happened and why."

"I need to do this, if that's okay with you. I've kept it to myself too long and it's killing me inside."

The urge to hug her was strong instead he nodded for her to continue.

"The next day, after he'd left, I packed up a few items, liquidated all the cash I could, and left. I'd already secured my dad's company so there was no way Brett could touch it, especially without marrying me. I used my money to find a way to purchase a new identity and I left. That was four hundred and thirty-two days ago."

Brandon looked at Wyatt. "There is no info on her because the identity has never been used for anything other than renting this place.

She doesn't have social media and doesn't use credit cards. When Carl came to me, questioning what he should do, I was able to find out who Norah was and after looking into it, I understood why. She needed a safe place to lay low, she wasn't dangerous and hadn't done anything illegal. He was content with that information and didn't want anything else. So I kept it to myself, keeping an eye on her to make sure all was well."

"You've known this whole time about all of it?"

"Not all but I'd found out who she really was and then when I did a little digging, found out about her fiance and all the things he was still doing to try to get control of the company."

He looked at Norah. "What's the company?"

"Eversware."

His mouth dropped open. "Eversware?"

She nodded.

Eversware was the biggest software company around. At the height of his career, the shares of the company were some of the most profitable. And then it hit him. "You're Norah Evers."

She didn't answer with a yes, instead looked up to him, almost shocked he'd known who she was.

"I used to be a stockbroker and did my homework on all the big companies so I could better do my job."

"I guess that makes sense."

"I'm still trying to take all this in. Was there a plan on how long to stay away or what? And how are you surviving?"

"I have plenty of money, although it is starting to dwindle since I can't put it into a bank to earn interest." She shrugged. "As for a plan, there wasn't really one. I just knew I had to get away and I'd rather give up everything than to have Brett take over or worse kill me."

Before he could speak again, Brandon interrupted. "I hate to do this, but I have to get going. There's an issue in town that I need to deal with."

Wyatt stood. "Thanks for helping out with this." He looked down to where Norah was still sitting on the couch. "I appreciate it."

"Anytime. And Norah, I'm here if you need anything and like I promised, I won't look into anything."

After he was gone, Wyatt asked her, "Why don't you want him to look into anything?"

"Because any search into me, the company or Brett could make Brett aware of where I am."

That made sense. "I guess I'll get going. Thank you for telling me your story. I'm sorry you had to dredge it all up again."

She stood quickly. "You don't have to leave if you don't want to." Her voice was almost frantic, like she was panicking.

"I just assumed you'd want me to go."

Her eyes searched his. "Do you have any idea how long it's been since I've had people to talk to? I'm about to go crazy here. In fact, today before this, I was on edge and sure I was finally going to break. Please don't leave me alone yet."

How the hell was he supposed to leave when she was practically begging him to stay.

Not that he wanted to leave.

"Unless you have work to do."

"I have nothing to do," he answered quickly. "I can stay." He moved back across the room, toward her.

"Will you...tell me about yourself? Actually, you could talk to me about the weather and I'd be happy. Anything at all would be fine."

Laughing, he sat back down. "I'm not that interesting but I can tell you about me."

She also sat back down. "A former stockbroker who now owns a building in a small town. At what, thirty years old? That's pretty interesting."

"I'm choosing to ignore the fact that you think I look thirty when I am obviously only twenty-six."

She gave a funny little smile, all her teeth showing. "I estimated high because I'm so used to people thinking I am younger than I am, and I hate it."

"That makes sense. You're what, twenty-five?"

"Only for a few more days. I turn twenty-six on Friday."

"Happy early birthday."

"This will be the second birthday that I celebrate alone. Not really happy."

Instantly, he wanted to make sure she didn't spend her birthday alone. He could get a cake and maybe Joy and Flynn could come. Anything to make her happy.

Anything.

"My last birthday was celebrated in the hospital, so being alone doesn't sound so bad."

"Oh my God, what happened?"

"It's part of my story, if you're really interested in hearing it?"

"I am and not just because I want the company. But because I am genuinely interested." Her eyes told him that she was being truthful.

Her beautiful, anything but plain, brown eyes.

They just didn't fit with her blonde hair but now that he knew who she was, he remembered that she'd always had dark brown hair.

"I've only been in Cedarville for about nine months. Before that I was in New York City where I was a stockbroker. Numbers have always been my thing and I'd always been good with picking the right companies to invest in. Even in high school, my dad always asked for my help with his investments. When it came time for college, it was the natural thing for me to get a business degree and then go into trading. For a few years I loved it but then it started to consume my life and I was working eighty hour weeks, barely eating or sleeping. The final straw was when I started to have daily panic attacks. It was just too stressful and I needed a change. So when I ended up in the hospital on my birthday due to stress and a panic attack, I was done."

"Why Cedarville?" She looked totally engrossed in his story.

"My brother lives here. Flynn. I really wanted to be around family but I didn't want to live in the town I grew up in. This was the logical choice."

"And how'd you come to buy this building?"

"I needed something, a way to make money and something to do. Flynn helped out and together we purchased it. With my money management skills, I had saved a lot which gave me the resources to buy both this building and the one in town where Joy's salon is."

"You own that too?"

"Yep. I hope to buy a few more in the future. I've found that owning something and making a difference in people's lives by making sure they have a roof over their heads, suits me."

"It's nice when you find something you love to do."

"Is that how it was with you? Before?"

She dropped her gaze down to her lap. "It was. I didn't love the software or business side but I loved running the charities and helping as many people as I could. I hated that when I left, I had to take money that would normally go to those in need."

"I remember reading about how Everware gave over half their profits away. It was one of the reasons the stock was popular. People like a company that does good deeds. You know they don't do that now right? The last year or so, they gave away only a tiny fraction."

"What?" Her head snapped up.

"I still keep up with stocks and companies for my own personal reasons and Eversware is not as popular as it once was." At her look of shock, he asked, "You didn't know?"

"I don't do searches for fear that Brett has some way to track it back to me. I only know what I see on TV."

"If you want, I could print out any info you might be interested in reading. It wouldn't be weird for me, because I am always searching companies. No red flags should be raised."

Her eyes widened. "You'd do that?"

"Sure. Or really, you could just come across the hall and read on my computer if you wanted."

"It should only be when you are actually searching for stuff that you'd normally do. Brett has a whole software company, and many hackers at his disposal. There's no idea what he could search or find."

"I'll make sure I don't do any extra searches. I promise."

"Thank you. I'm sure you think I'm paranoid. Hell most of the time I think I'm paranoid but I'm not willing to chance him finding me."

"I don't think you're paranoid. I think what you did is pretty amazing. You had to be scared shitless and yet you still did it."

"I wish I felt amazing. Most days I just feel like a person who is losing her mind." She laughed. "Hey can I ask you something?"

Please let it be a hug or something else that would allow him to touch her. "Shoot."

"You said that Flynn was your brother right? But you guys look nothing alike. Granted I haven't met him, but I've seen him and Joy has shown me pictures."

Not a hug but that she wanted to know more about him was a good thing. He hoped. "That's an easy one. Both Flynn and I are adopted."

"Oh, I...didn't know."

"I wouldn't have suspected you to. It's not a secret though and neither Flynn or I mind talking about it. Our parents, the adopted ones, are amazing and we love making sure people know."

"That's sweet."

Sweet. She thought he was sweet. "Mom hates it but dad secretly gets a kick out of it."

"You're lucky to have them."

"I couldn't agree more." His phone buzzed in his pocket and he pulled it out to check it. "I need to take this."

"Go ahead." She stood and walked into her small kitchen.

He answered the call, which was one of the tenants.

After a short discussion, he hung up. "I'm gonna have to head out. Mr. and Mrs. Cannon are having an issue with their electricity and I need to head upstairs to check on it."

"Oh sure. I'm sorry I kept you so long." She walked back to the living area.

"I liked talking to you." He didn't want to scare her, but he really wanted to keep talking to her. "Maybe we can do it again?"

Her eyes widened. "I would love that. Being stuck inside all the time, I was starting to worry that I had lost my ability to socialize."

"You haven't. Or at least I don't think you have. I'm not much better when it comes to being around people. This town has helped me but I'm still awkward."

A smile tilted her lips upward. "You don't seem awkward to me."

He walked towards the door. "Enjoy the rest of your day and Norah, thank you for telling me your story. I hate that you had to but it helps to know it."

She nodded silently as he pulled the door open. With one last look back at her, he left, closing the door behind him.

As soon as he was in the hall, he closed his eyes, and touched a hand to his heart. Everything about her drew him in. What she had gone through, and how she had dealt with it made her strong and he found that extremely appealing. So appealing that he was having a hard time walking away from her.

Something that had never happened to him before.

Chapter 4

Alone again, Norah felt behind her for the couch to make sure she didn't fall to the floor.

Wyatt was...well he was dreamy.

It was weird. She'd never used that word before to describe a man. Never felt it was warranted. But with Wyatt that was the only way to describe him. It was like if you took all the best parts of every fairytale prince and combined them.

You'd get Wyatt.

The dark hair that he ran his fingers through. The dark eyes that felt as if they could see into her soul. His lean muscular build that had her fingers twitching to run over them. His deep voice, that held concern when he spoke.

It was all overwhelming.

But tempting.

Her assumption was that he had a girlfriend but that didn't mean she couldn't daydream about him.

Or you know, dream while in bed.

When Chief Graham, or Brandon as he'd asked her to call him, had knocked on her door, she'd almost had a heart attack. But he'd been amazing. Spoke softly and with purpose telling her that she didn't need to be afraid but that he knew who she was.

Before she'd even had the chance to panic and think the worst, he'd kept talking, telling her how he'd found out and why he was there. He hadn't been there to take her back, Brett hadn't sent him.

He was there because he was concerned and because her new landlord was questioning why there wasn't a background check in her file.

He'd assured her over and over again that she was safe in Cedarville and that he'd do everything in his power to keep it that way.

For the first time in over a year, she'd felt like there was someone on her side. She told him her story and when she was finished he'd asked if she was comfortable with her landlord, Wyatt knowing everything she'd told him.

She nodded but had no idea he was going to bring him into her apartment to make her tell the story again.

She was glad he had though.

Just Wyatt's presence had made her feel secure and then when Brandon had left and they'd kept talking, it was easy.

Easier than it had ever been talking to anyone other than her mom or dad.

And it wasn't that she'd been shy or unconfident in her old life. Just the opposite really. She was able to head up huge events and raise hundreds of thousands of dollars for charity. She'd sat in meetings with some of the most powerful people in the world.

But with Wyatt, there had been no pretense, no power struggle and she hadn't wanted anything from him.

She was just herself and it'd felt easy. And right.

It was possible that she was only feeling this way due to her lack of human contact the last year though. What did it even matter anyway? The man had to have a girlfriend. He was too damn good looking to be single.

She wanted to know more about him. More about how old he was when he was adopted or how it shaped his life. More about the stress that caused him to move to Cedarville.

Just more about everything.

Rolling her eyes at her own thoughts, she stood up. Because Brandon had shown up during lunch, she'd yet to eat and now that she thought about it, she was hungry.

She rummaged through her kitchen looking for something only to realize that she was running low on a few items. She kept her kitchen and everything else for that matter, overstocked most of the time.

Generally she made a run to the store once a week with a few exceptions here and there.

Those were the only times she left her apartment.

But as she stood and looked through her fridge, she caught herself craving a big-ass burger from a restaurant.

She hadn't had cravings in months. But it was because of all the weirdness of her day that was making her crave it.

Could she chance going out to get one? Better yet, should she?

Where would she even go?

She wasn't familiar with a lot of the best places in town since she didn't go to them. Oh there was a place Joy was always talking about that her friend owned.

But she couldn't remember the name.

Finding her phone, she texted Joy to find out the name.

Norah:

What is the name of the restaurant your friend owns that you always eat at?

Joy:

Dockside. Are you planning to go?

Norah:

I'd really like a burger and thinking I might.

Maybe it was also time to tell her friend why she was there and why she rarely left her apartment. Brandon knew and now so did Wyatt. Would one more person matter so much?

It probably wouldn't be a big deal but she didn't think she could. At least not yet.

Joy:

If you plan to go, give me a heads up and I'll let Wes know.

Norah:

I will, thank you.

Butterflies consumed her stomach at just the thought of going out for something other than supplies. It had been too long and once wouldn't hurt. She could wear a hat and maybe a big hoodie and coat. She would be unrecognizable.

Plus it was the middle of the day. How busy could it be?

Practically running to her room, she changed into boring clothes — which really was all she had these days — found a baseball hat that she pulled low on her head covering her face, and threw on some gym shoes.

She was going out for a hamburger.

It was almost too exciting.

With her purse wrapped around her body, she opened her door to walk out. But stepping through was harder than she thought. She did it though, locking the door behind her. She had to literally force herself to take the five steps to the front door. What was wrong with her? She left her apartment once a week and never had any troubles.

But she couldn't force herself to open the front door and walk through it.

"Norah."

She heard her name, knew it was Wyatt's voice but could do nothing but stare at the glass door.

"Norah, is everything okay?" This time he walked up behind her, standing what felt like only inches from her body.

"I was craving a burger, and thought I could do it. Figured it would be no big deal. But I can't make myself walk out the door." Her voice cracked and she knew that soon tears would flow down her cheeks.

"Why don't we go back into your apartment for a second." She felt his hand on her shoulder, a warmth suddenly streaming through her whole body.

She turned her head, looking up at his face. "I can't seem to move." It was the truth. She couldn't move forward nor could she go backward.

She was stuck.

Just like in life.

"It's okay, I can help." His hands gripped her shoulders, steering her backward. She was in a daze and not really paying attention to what was happening. She felt herself moving, felt his hands on her shoulders, felt her tears on her skin.

But that was it.

After who knows how long, she became aware of her surroundings. She was sitting on a couch, but not her couch. Looking around, she noticed the place looked similar to her apartment, just a little bigger. Finally, her eyes landed on Wyatt, who was standing in his kitchen.

"Is this...your place?"

"It is, I hope that's okay? You were kinda out of it and I wanted to get you sitting as fast as possible."

She blinked several times, the tears still falling only slower. Wiping her cheeks with the back of her hand, she nodded. "I don't know what's wrong with me."

He came around the counter, two bottles of water in his hands. "You've had an intense day and then on top of it, you were trying to go out into the world. Something you barely do."

He sat down next to her, handing her a bottle of water. "I just wanted a burger."

"I can understand that. I'm not sure how I would survive without a greasy cheeseburger every now and then."

"I thought I could do it. After talking to Brandon and then to you, I thought I could walk out of here on a non scheduled day, go somewhere I've never been, and eat a burger." She lifted her arms, dropping them quickly. "I'm so tired."

"I can help you get home so you can sleep."

His face held so much concern. "Not that kind of tired. Just tired of how I'm living." She gave a strangled laugh. "Who am I kidding, this isn't living. It's barely surviving."

"Are you kidding? What you did, leaving a man who was abusive and possibly worse, that's the purest form of survival. You made a decision to give up everything you had including your identity and left. That makes you strong whether you realize it or not."

His hand had reached out and was now sitting on top of hers. It felt good, better than good. She couldn't remember the last time she'd been touched let alone comforted. "You may think that, but it's not how it feels to me. I'm starting to think that I just ran away because I couldn't do it anymore."

"Listen, I didn't want to say this earlier because I didn't want to freak you out, but your ex, Brett Dalton, he is not a great guy. Eversware has always been a stock I loved. Family company, great values, I have invested a lot of my own money in it. So I keep up with news of the company and I get shareholder info. A lot has changed and he is the reason. Not to mention his pleas for you to return home, well they never did sit well with me. It always looked like he was smiling and his words came out as cocky. Not like a man who was in love and afraid his fiance was hurt."

"What are you saying?" She searched his face, needing more.

"I'm saying that you did the right thing. That man is bad. Bad to the point that I'm fearing for your life and I just met you."

Because she needed it, she turned her palm upward, wrapping her fingers around his hand. "So I didn't run for no reason?"

"No, in my opinion you ran for the right reasons."

His hand felt so good in hers that she didn't make a move to pull away. And shockingly, neither did he.

"You know, if you want, I could go get you a burger? In fact, I could place a whole order that includes the best homemade fries you've ever eaten, not to mention cupcakes."

"You'd do that?"

"Sure, that's what we do in Cedarville. We help each other out."

It stung a little to know that he was only helping her out because it was the right thing to do. She'd rather there be another reason.

Like maybe he wanted to rip her clothes off and have his way with her.

That would be a much better reason.

But unlikely.

Although she would love to rip her own clothes off and then never wear the ugly things again. All she owned were plain, boring clothes. And very few at that. She hadn't wanted to spend her money on clothes when no one ever saw her.

"I hate to put you out."

"Not a problem. I haven't eaten yet either and a burger from Dockside sounds just about perfect." He stood. "Why don't you wait here and I'll go get the food."

"You want me to stay here?"

"I thought it might be a nice change of pace from your place." His eyes were dancing with humor.

"Oh yeah, because they are completely different."

Laughing, he walked to the kitchen where she watched him pocket his keys. "Well, mine is a lot dirtier."

She looked around. It didn't seem dirty to her. "Looks clean to me."

"Only because you haven't seen my bathroom yet." He walked to the door. "Want everything on the burger."

Just thinking about it had her salivating. "Yes."

"I'll be back in less than twenty minutes. Make yourself at home."

She watched him walk out the door, leaving a virtual stranger alone in his apartment.

The man was either very trusting or insane.

What he definitely was, was hot.

When he was sitting close to her, their hands touching, her eyes looking into his...God she wanted to melt. Whether he did or not, it felt like he actually cared. Like he wanted to be next to her.

Something that had never happened to her with another man.

Slumping back into the couch, she laughed out loud. She was delusional. Being alone had made her insane. Wyatt was just being nice, he in no way wanted anything more from her.

She'd just have to keep him in her dreams where he belonged.

Chapter 5

He was shaking. Actually shaking as he drove to Dockside.

That's what she did to him.

After having contact with her twice.

It was official. He was insane.

Never in his life had a woman so completely enthralled him this quickly. From the first second he'd walked into her apartment to see her sitting on her couch, he'd been in deep. Then he'd heard her story, finding out all she'd done just to survive and he'd dug his hole deeper.

When he'd found her standing at the front door, frozen with tears running down her cheeks, he'd wanted nothing more than to take her into his arms to comfort her.

And when he'd absently set his hand on top of hers while they'd been talking, a calming feeling had come over him. Then she'd turned her hand in his, entwining their fingers and his heart had flipped in his chest.

All he'd wanted at that moment was for her to be happy. And if a cheeseburger would do that, he was going to be the one to make it happen. Hell if she wanted one everyday, he'd drive to get her one.

Or buy a grill and make her one.

Whatever she wanted.

He'd do all of it.

Which was why he was shaking. He'd never been in this situation before. Never felt literal sparks when he'd touched someone. Never felt like breathing came second to making her happy.

This out of control feeling was similar to his previous panic attacks only there was no panic. The panic only set in when he thought about her not liking him. And that was more of a wanting to vomit kind of panic, not a can't breath panic.

There was a problem though. He couldn't pursue her. She was in a precarious situation and the last thing she needed was a man. A man is what caused the situation. And sure, he wasn't her ex, would never hit or even mentally abuse a woman, but she didn't know that.

He was a stranger to her.

But he was going to fix that.

If he couldn't be anything else, he could at least be her friend.

Pulling into Dockside, he shut off his car before hopping out and running inside. He'd texted in an order to Wes as soon as he'd left his apartment and he wanted to get back to Norah as quickly as possible.

The place wasn't too busy, which made sense since it was after lunch and before dinner. He found Patrick behind the bar.

Normally Patrick worked in the kitchen and the head bartender, Sabrina worked the bar.

"You serving drinks now?" he asked as he walked up.

"Today I am. Sabrina needed the day off so I volunteered to take her shift."

"I placed a to go order with Wes."

"Yeah he's back there now finishing it up. I boxed up the cupcakes." He slid the box across the counter but stopped before Wyatt could grab the box. "Planning on telling me who you ordered that food for?"

"Why can't it be for me?"

"It could, but one, I have never seen you place a take out order from here and two, you ordered a half dozen cupcakes. You never order dessert."

He snatched the box from his friend. "You should be happy I'm ordering cupcakes since it's your girlfriend who makes them." Dani and Patrick had been together for about three months and the woman could bake. She had the whole town addicted to sugar.

And Patrick addicted to her.

"While I always appreciate the support of the woman I love, I also want to know what is going on?"

"I'm just buying lunch for a friend."

"A female friend?" He raised his eyebrows.

Wyatt glared at him. "You know, I'm starting to understand Flynn saying this town is like a big family. Everyone is fucking nosy."

He was saved when Wes walked out from the kitchen carrying a bag he assumed was his order. "Here ya go." He said, handing him the bag.

"Thanks, man." He slid Patrick his credit card. "Appreciate the quick work."

"Late lunch?"

"Ah yeah. I got busy and forgot."

"You and someone else?" Wes was smiling like he knew something.

"Okay gossip girls. Yes, I am having a meal with a woman. No, I am not going to tell you who." Patrick handed his card back to him along with a receipt that he signed. "You can all go back to doing whatever it was you were doing before I showed up." He took the box of cupcakes, along with the bag of food and left.

Cedarville really was a town where everyone wanted to know everything.

And while he hated it when they were focused on him, overall he loved it. At least people cared. In New York, no one had given a damn. Everyone was out for themselves and for someone who grew up in a small town, that was hard.

He made it home in record speed, thanks to very little traffic. When he entered his apartment, he had no idea what to expect. But it sure wasn't what he found.

She was lounging on his couch, her bare feet sticking out from under the blanket that his mom had made him right before he'd left for college.

"Hi," she said brightly when he entered. "That was fast."

"It's close," he said and closed the door behind him trying hard not to stare at how right she looked under his blanket.

He was never washing that thing again.

She dropped her legs to the floor, pushing the blanket off her. "That smells amazing." Standing, she joined him at the kitchen counter. "Hey

Wyatt." Her voice was quiet, almost a whisper. "Thank you. For all this. The food, the place to get away and most of all for listening."

He was lost in her eyes. "It was all my pleasure."

"I'd hate to find out what you do for fun if dealing with me was a pleasure."

He started unpacking the food. "Until recently, I didn't really have fun. I worked and worked and worked some more."

"But you've been here a year right? There has to be something you do?"

He walked to the cabinet and grabbed two plates. "In this town there is always something going on. A party, or festival or lately, weddings. It keeps me pretty busy."

"You've made a lot of friends then?"

"I guess. Everyone around here is really nice and since Flynn is with Joy and Joy's sister, Avery is with Dax who is also Flynn's boss, it means I get built in friends."

"Joy used to scare me when I first met her. She was so outgoing that I was afraid she would question why I rarely left my apartment. But she never did. Instead she started dropping by to chat or ask for advice. It felt so good to finally have a friend."

"Joy is like that. A force of nature really. And seriously other than Flynn, I think most people were afraid of her when they first met her."

"I love hearing her talk about how much she loves Flynn. It's inspiring."

"At first I thought Flynn was crazy. Chasing after a woman who obviously didn't want him. But after I met her and then saw them together, it was easy to see that she did want him but was just fighting with herself."

"Is Flynn older than you?"

Their food was plated and each of them took a seat to start eating. "He's four years older. He was eight when I was adopted."

"Was that hard? Being adopted?"

He looked at her, wondering why she wanted to know anything about him. Most people didn't ask about his adoption almost like they felt he wouldn't want to talk about it. But he didn't care. Being adopted was the best thing that had ever happened to him and he loved talking about his family. "The first few months were hard because I kept thinking I was going to be sent away again. Flynn was the only one I trusted and because of that, I never left his side."

She stopped eating, the burger halfway to her mouth. "When did you finally realize that you weren't going to be sent away?"

"The story Flynn tells is that it was about a month after being there. He had to go to school but I was freaking out that he was leaving. So my mom sits down next to me and asks what if she stays home with me. And then my dad did the same thing. And for a week, both of them stayed home with me while Flynn was at school. By the end of that week, I no longer followed only Flynn around, but also them."

"That is the sweetest story. They sound like amazing people."

"They are and I am so lucky they picked me. There is not one day that goes by that I don't think about what my life could be if not for them."

"I do the same with my parents. I grew up as a wealthy kid who never wanted for anything. But when I started volunteering, I became aware of just how lucky I was. There are kids who have no one and parent's who want to do right by their kids but just don't have the money or resources. It broke my heart and I couldn't sit by and do nothing."

"From what I know, you did a lot of good."

"I tried. I really did. And my mom and dad were completely on board. They hadn't grown up wealthy. They'd both come from lower to middle class families where they had to work for every penny they had. To them, having that kind of money was a burden if you didn't do any good in the world."

"I'd say you were lucky to have them just as much as I was lucky to have mine."

Her face fell. "I miss them so much."

Her voice broke him. "Norah, I am so sorry. I didn't mean to make you sad."

She wiped her eyes as if afraid to let him see the tears. "No, I like talking about them. For a long time now I never had anyone to talk about them to. It feels good to mention them. Like I didn't forget them."

"You will never forget them. They are a part of you always." He laid his hand on top of hers on the counter. It felt so good to touch her, to hopefully comfort her a little.

"God, I'm a mess." She sniffed, shaking her head. "You didn't ask for any of this. You're trying to be stress free and I am so full of stress."

"You aren't causing me any stress, Norah. I want to help you. I wouldn't want to be anywhere else but right here listening to you talk about your parents. Or your crazy ex. Or really anything. If you wanted to talk about frogs, I would pull out my phone and Google them just so I had something to talk to you about."

As soon as he stopped talking he realized that he might have said too much. Her eyes were wide, her mouth gaping open.

"I didn't mean —" his words were cut off when her lips pressed against his. It was quick, so quick that it was over before he could even register it.

But he did register it and his whole body was on fire. Her lips against his was the best thing he could ever remember feeling.

Ever.

"I'm so sorry." She touched her fingers to her lips. "I didn't mean to do that. You were just being nice and I've been alone so long." She shrugged. "I didn't mean anything by it."

Still stunned, he said nothing.

"I barely know you. You might even have a girlfriend. God I am so stupid." She started to turn in her chair but he reached for her, his hand on her elbow.

"I don't have a girlfriend." His words were direct, making sure she understood what he was saying.

"Still," she bit her bottom lip, "I shouldn't have done that."

"It was..." he wanted to say fantastic, amazing, the best thing that had ever happened to him, but instead went with, "nice."

Great job, idiot, way to make it sound like she'd given him a cup of coffee.

Her dark eyes lightened, shining in the light that was coming in through his sliding glass door. "It was nice. And as much as I should be, I'm not really sorry. I think I just needed to feel something."

Well that sucked. She had only used him to make herself feel. "Glad I could help.

She reached out, her hand touching his chest. The heat of her palm was evident even through his long sleeved t-shirt. "I didn't mean it like that. I'm pretty sure that if you had been any other guy, it wouldn't have happened. You just...well you make me feel strong. Something no guy other than my dad has ever made me feel."

He softened. "You are strong. Never doubt that."

Her palm lingered for a few more seconds and when she moved it, the loss was immediately noticeable to him. They started eating again, both of them silent as they ate their food. He watched as she polished off her burger and fries in record speed. When he pushed the rest of his fries toward her, she tried to push them back.

"Eat them please. I get them all the time."

Her puppy dog look of thankfulness almost unraveled him. "They're so good. I can't remember ever eating fries this good."

"Wes makes them from scratch everyday."

"He's got a gift." She dipped each fry in ketchup before enthusiastically popping it into her mouth.

God what he'd give to be that fry.

"I can bring you some whenever you want. I go to Dockside several times a week." He'd do anything she asked if it meant spending more time with her.

"I could never ask you to do that. Plus, it's not in my budget to buy restaurant food all the time."

"Do you mind if I ask how you are surviving? Money wise?"

She wiped her hands on her napkin. "I was able to get around four hundred thousand dollars when I left. But since I can't invest it or earn interest, it's dwindling fast."

"Yeah, I can see how that would be a problem."

"I had no plan when I left, I just knew I needed to get away. Now though, I wish I had thought ahead and taken more." She stood, picking up their plates and taking them into his kitchen. "I have no idea when, if ever I'll be able to go back to my former life."

He stood, collecting the boxes the food had come in. "You can't live this way forever."

"I know and I don't really want to. I loved my life. Loved how many people I helped. But without my parents," she shrugged looking at him over her shoulder, "sometimes I think there's nothing there to go back to."

His heart, which already wanted her to stay in Cedarville forever, was happy at her confession but his mind knew better. It knew she would regret it if she never went back to California to face what she left behind. It wasn't his place to say so though.

"That can't be true. You had a whole life there, people who counted on you or loved you."

She slid the last dish into his dishwasher, closed it and then leaned back against it. "You'd think right? But there is not one person who I miss. Not one. Isn't that odd? I'm in my mid twenties and yet I have no real relationships with anyone and the one I did have turned out to be abusive."

"Until moving here, I wasn't much better. Like you I had my family but there wasn't anyone else that I would call a close friend. No one I would call on a Friday night to go get drinks with or someone to go to a ball game with. I socialized but that was all it was. I had no real friends. Then I came here and that changed almost immediately. And you know what, I realized that I'd been missing out. Friends are a good thing."

"That sounds nice, I just don't think that will happen to me."

"Why not. You have Joy, she's your friend right? And now me. We could be friends." Or more but he wasn't about to say that.

Her head snapped up. "You'd want that? To be my friend?"

"Are you kidding? I'd love to be your friend. Added benefit, you live right across the hall so I don't have to drive anywhere to see you." He grinned, winking to let her know he was joking.

"Your promise to bring me fries is all I need. "

Her easy sense of humor, even after all she'd been through, was sexy as hell. "Go ahead, use me for my fries."

She dropped her head back, laughing. Her neck was long and inviting, forcing him to walk back around the counter to get away from her.

Being just her friend was not going to be easy when his heart, and let's face it, dick, wanted so much more.

Chapter 6

Wallowing, that's what she was doing.

Two days ago she'd had the best day since she'd gone into hiding. Honestly it might have been the best day she'd had ever. It had sure felt like it. But since then, nothing.

Well not nothing. He'd texted her twice just saying hi, asking how she was. That was it though. He didn't stop by or bring her fries or anything.

Meaning once again she was all alone.

He probably thought she was a crazy person. She'd kissed him for God's sake. If she'd been on the receiving end of that, she'd run for her life too.

Actually, if he'd kissed her, she'd have probably thrown him to the ground and had her way with him.

Maybe then she wouldn't be so pent up.

Somehow it had felt wrong to take care of the problem herself now that they were friends. But maybe they weren't friends. Had he just said that to shut her up?

She needed to put him out of her mind. A puzzle, she could do a puzzle. Standing she went to her closet to pick when, when she heard a knock on her door. Her first instinct was to run toward it to see if it was Wyatt. But because that felt crazy, she did the opposite.

Looking through her peephole, instead of Wyatt she found Joy.

"Hi," she said as she opened the door.

"Special delivery," she said and held up a bag that smelled amazing."

"What's that?"

"Burger and fries from Dockside. Wyatt, had me get them for you."

So he hadn't forgotten about her. "Come in." She moved out of the way, letting Joy walk past her.

"What I want to know is why has Wyatt texted me four times to make sure I bring you food?"

He'd asked her four times? "I don't know."

"I call bullshit. When he texted me yesterday and I didn't have enough time, he was pissed. Then today, he kept hounding me until I finally said I was on my way."

"Where is he?"

"He didn't tell you?"

"No, I haven't seen him since Monday."

"Both he and Flynn went to Indiana because their mom was having a biopsy on her breast. They wanted to be there for her."

Her hand automatically went to her mouth. "Oh no, is she okay?"

"Yeah the results came back today and it was benign. They plan to head home tomorrow."

"That's great news." After only talking to him for a few hours, she knew how much he loved his mom.

"It is. I really wanted to go, but there was no way for me to make it work. Their mom is one of my favorite people and I've only met her once."

"I'm sure she understands."

"She did." There was a long pause. "Are you ready to tell me what's up with you and Wyatt?"

"There's nothing up. We met the other day and because he's a nice guy, he offered to bring me fries whenever I wanted them."

"He is a nice guy and that sounds like something he'd do. You know what isn't something he'd do? Texting me four times to make sure it's done."

She sat silently, unable to answer her friend.

"Is there something going on?"

"No," her voice was low. "We are just friends."

"Norah, you know you can talk to me. Just because I am virtually related to Wyatt doesn't mean I would tell him anything that we talked about. Also, I might love his brother but I'm not immune to his good looks. The man is seriously hot."

Norah felt the smile come of its own accord. "He is pretty easy on the eyes."

"Don't I know it. Flynn hates it so I make sure to bring it up all the time."

"You are horrible." She opened the bag sitting in front of her, and popped a fry into her mouth. "We are just friends, that much is true. But there is a lot you don't know about me."

"And Wyatt knows those things?"

She nodded, grabbing another fry.

"You don't have to tell me, I'm just glad you have someone."

"I think I'd like to tell you, if you have time." She was surprisingly calm, much more than when she'd told Brandon and Wyatt.

"I have time but again, you don't need to tell me anything. We are friends no matter what."

She wondered if she'd ever had a friend who thought like that. One who didn't care about her money or who her parents were. Was there anyone who had ever just liked her for her?

"Do you know of the company Eversware?" That was the easiest place to start.

"Sure, who doesn't."

"My name isn't Norah Baker, it's Norah Evers." She left it hanging because like Brandon and Wyatt, Joy was smart and would probably figure it out on her own.

"Holy shit! I've heard of you. You disappeared a while ago and people think you are dead."

She nodded. "I'm obviously not dead but that was kinda the hope that people would think I was and not come looking for me."

"But why?"

"My parents died and shortly after my fiance, who worked for the company, started to change. He became angry, demanding and aggressive. The emotional abuse was a lot and the last straw was when he struck me during an argument. During that fight he also insinuated that he'd made sure my parents were out of the way. Which I took to mean he'd had something to do with their deaths."

Joy's eyes went wide and her mouth dropped open. "Mother fucker. I hope you reported him?"

"I did, but the police said I had no evidence. They did question him though but that only pissed him off more and he threatened to kill me. I saw no other choice but to leave. I left everything behind, but took what I hoped was enough cash to survive. I bought a new identity and got out of there as fast as I could."

"You are so brave."

Those words made her head snap up. "Brave? I ran away."

"You got out of a situation that could have killed you. That's not running. That's bravery."

She'd never really looked at it like that. Wyatt had said something similar but she'd just shrugged it off as something people say when hearing a story like hers. "I wish I felt brave. Most days I just feel like a lonely coward."

Joy reached out, touching her arm. "You aren't alone here. You have me and Wyatt and there could be others if you wanted. I haven't been here that long. Only since March and already I have more real friends than I have ever had. And believe me," she raised an eyebrow, "I was not looking for friends. I liked being alone. But that's not really how it works here."

"I'm just afraid of showing my face too much. If Brett ever finds me, I'm afraid of what will happen."

"I think we can work around that. We can make sure you are never alone if we are out and most of the time we hang out at someone's house anyway."

"But what about when I'm here? He could follow me."

"This place is secure. Locked entry, cameras, I don't think he could get by the security but even if he did, Wyatt is right next door. And from the texts he's been sending me, I am pretty sure he would protect you."

Biting her lip, she wondered if that was true. Would he protect her? More importantly, why? Yes she had her absurd fantasies about him but that didn't mean he felt the same.

"It would be nice to have company other than myself sometimes."

"How about we start this Friday night? Flynn and I will have a few people over, not everyone so we don't overwhelm you, but a couple. What do you think?"

She was nervous to say yes, but she was sick to death of staring at the walls in her apartment. "Promise it won't be too many people?"

"No more than eight or ten."

She nodded. "Okay, that could work."

Joy stood. "I'll text you all the info. I'm sure I can twist Wyatt's arm to drive you." She shook her head, chuckling. "And don't worry, I won't tell anyone your story."

"Thank you. And thanks for the food. You're a good friend."

She opened the door. "I wasn't always. Sometime I'll tell you my story. It'll shock you to find out that I haven't always been this amazing." She left, closing the door behind her.

Norah wondered what Joy was talking about. She couldn't imagine her as anything other than what she was now.

She sat back down to finish her food just as a text dinged on her phone.

Picking it up, she saw it was Wyatt and her heart did a little flip.

Wyatt:

I hope Joy was able to bring you some food. I unexpectedly had to go out of town but I'm almost home and if she didn't, I can bring you something.

Dumbfounded that anyone let alone a man could care so much, she held her phone to her chest. She wasn't used to anyone caring about her so much. Well that wasn't totally true. Her parents had been that way.

They had always put her first, making sure she felt loved and taken care of.

Norah:

Thank you for thinking of me at all. Joy just left and I am eating some amazing fries as I type this.

Wyatt:

If I told you that I thought of you a lot, would that be okay?

Norah:

It would make me wonder if you had a head injury since I'm nothing special.

Wyatt:

Do me a favor okay and stop thinking like that. You are special. And smart and funny and brave. Definitely brave. And beautiful.

She sighed as she read his words over and over. The superficial part of her loved that he said she was beautiful. She didn't feel beautiful with her bleached blonde hair, lack of make up and baggy clothes. She had never been a person to care about looks but back then, she had her own dark hair that she had cut at a fancy salon and clothes that actually fit. She purposely bought her clothes big when she'd left so that she'd blend in public.

But now, she wished she was a little bit of her old self.

She debated texting him back but what could she say? There was nothing. Instead she ate her food, wrote a little and then settled into her couch for a late afternoon nap. She was on the verge of falling asleep when she heard the outside door to the complex slam shut. Jumping from the couch, she ran to her door and without thinking or even looking through the peephole, she pulled her door open.

There standing a few feet in front of her at his door, was Wyatt. He turned as soon as he heard her, his smile lighting up his whole face.

"Norah." His voice was deep and sensual making her wonder if that's how it would sound if they were in bed.

"Wyatt." Her own was raspy like she was having trouble breathing.

They stared at each other intensely neither moving.

She could feel the heat between them and unless she was mistaken, he could too. And then he moved, so fast that she barely saw it coming. But that didn't stop her from meeting him halfway. She wanted him to know that it wasn't just him, that she wanted the kiss just as much.

Their lips crashed together with his arms going around her body. And thank God they did because there was no way she was steady enough to stay upright. His lips were soft as they moved against hers and when his tongue darted out and into her mouth, she wondered if a kiss had ever been so all consuming.

Their tongues tangled as his hands tightened on her lower back. She heard him moan or maybe it was her. Who knows. But it didn't matter. They were both in this, right where they wanted to be.

"Norah," he whispered against her neck as his lips moved down, teasing her even more.

"Don't stop please," she begged. She hated how needy she sounded but she hadn't felt this good in forever and it was more than just lack of companionship.

It was Wyatt.

"I promise to start back up again but we have to get out of this hallway."

He was right, she knew it but that didn't stop her from pressing in closer to his body.

"Goddammit!" he swore, pushing her away. "Don't move." He turned, unlocked his door, opened it to throw his bag inside and then pulled it closed. Facing her again, he pointed. "Inside."

His voice, expression and stance all turned her on. If he had told her to strip right there, she was pretty sure she would have done it. Following his orders, she moved into her apartment, him following right behind and shutting the door behind him.

She turned to look at him, her body humming with excitement. She wanted to speak but what did you say to the man you barely knew yet made out in a hallway with?

He took a step closer to her. "Tell me this is what you want?"

She swallowed the lump in her throat. "Wasn't it obvious?"

He stopped walking, closing his eyes. "I'm not sure I trust my instincts around you." His eyes opened. "You scatter my brain."

She laughed. "And you don't think you scatter mine?"

He reached for her, his fingers entwining with hers. "This feels crazy."

"I know, for me too."

"Maybe we shouldn't rush it. Take it slow."

"That's probably a good idea." She searched his eyes wondering if that was really how he felt.

He stepped even closer, his other hand reaching up and brushing against her cheek. "Slow doesn't mean we can't kiss."

She smiled, her own thoughts mirroring his. "Very good point." Taking the initiative, she pulled his mouth down to meet hers. Feeling his lips again had her on fire. She wanted more but knew he was right. Slow was better.

So ever so slowly, she tortured both of them with a slow kiss where she took her time, tasting him and learning him. Her hands took their time moving up his arms, the ones that held onto her waist, and when she reached his chest, she gripped his sweatshirt in her fists.

The kiss went on and on, seeming to last forever. Which was fine by her. When they finally came apart, she noticed that his cheeks were flushed and he was breathing heavily.

Same as her.

"I'm starting to think that crazy isn't so bad." He leaned his forehead against hers. "If this is what it gets me."

"I can do crazy." She let go of his shirt that was bunched in her fist and stepped back. "How was your trip?" She walked away, needing space if she was supposed to not jump him.

"Good. Great actually." He sat down on her couch. "My mom was having a biopsy on her breast and both Flynn and I wanted to be there."

"Joy mentioned it, I hope that's not a problem."

"Not at all. I wanted to tell you but I wasn't sure if you'd think that was weird with us just starting to be friends."

"I wouldn't have thought it was weird." She got in her fridge to grab some water. She wanted to tell him that she'd been sad that he hadn't stopped by or texted more but instead kept it to herself. "I'm glad your mom is okay."

"Yeah, it was nerve racking waiting for the results but it's benign and all is well."

"You're a good son." She stayed at the counter, opting to sit on a stool rather than go sit on the couch with him.

"Mom kept insisting that we didn't need to come which is why she tried to hide it from us but when dad let it slip, Flynn and I weren't about to not be there."

"I'm sure she was glad to see you."

"Yeah, it's been awhile. I didn't realize how much I missed them." He titled his head at her. "Why are you sitting so far away?"

"Honest answer?"

"Always."

"I'm afraid of what I'll do if I'm right next to you."

He let out a huge breath. "Oh good. I thought it was that you were afraid of me or were regretting the kissing."

"Never. I can't regret something that I want so badly."

"Do you think..." he paused like he wasn't sure what to say.

"Do I think what?"

"Do you think it's because you have been alone so long and not because it's me?"

"No!" She practically jumped off her stool. "I wondered the same thing but then I thought about it and realized that it's all you." She moved to the couch, sitting down right next to him. "I have a secret."

"Another one?"

"This one is about you." She looked down to her lap and said the words fast so she could get them out. "Before Monday, I thought about you."

"How can that be, we'd never met?"

"But I'd seen you and well, you know what you look like. But I always assumed it was just a surface crush. Then I met you on Monday and you blew all that to hell. You were...are...nice and sweet and funny. It was all I could do to stop thinking about you. And when I kissed you Monday...that wasn't just because I needed to feel something. It was because of you and how I was feeling about you."

"Can I tell you a secret?"

"Since you know all mine, you might as well."

"That kiss on Monday, was possibly the best one of my entire life. Until today."

"That can't be true. Not to sound like a broken record but have you seen yourself?"

He shrugged. "Yes I've had women come onto me just because of my looks but no one, and I mean no one, has ever taken the time to just talk to me. Ask what I like or what my hopes and dreams are. So when you kissed me, as chaste as it was, it was better than anything that had come before."

"I wish I knew what to do or say. I used to be good at this. Dating or flirting at least. But now, not only does it not come easy, it feels weird. I don't want to leave you guessing. I want you to know what I want. What I'm thinking."

He moved in closer. "What are you thinking?"

"That you should kiss me again." And he did. For long minutes they just kissed. Sensual, fast, hard. They ran the gamut over and over again.

And when he left, she fell onto her couch, happier than she'd been in forever.

They hadn't talked about what this was or what was going to happen but it didn't matter. She liked him. A lot. And it seemed he felt the same way. Together they would figure it out.

After a lot more kissing.

Chapter 7

Sleeping proved useless.

All his body wanted was Norah. He'd tried fixing the problem himself, but even that hadn't worked.

While he could get hard, or in his case stay hard just thinking about her, his release was nowhere in sight.

Norah was the only thing that would cure what ailed him.

Getting out of bed he saw that it was only four. Too early to head into town or to do any work on the building. That only left paperwork. And by paperwork, he meant working on his investments which gave him a good excuse to look into Eversware and the psychopath she was running from.

After just a few clicks, he was on his favorite website for tips and tricks about stocks. They always had information on the companies which helped investors make good decisions. And it looked like he was in luck. Right on the front page was a new article about Eversware.

He scanned it looking for any info that would pertain to Norah. There was nothing though. Just general company info. Clicking over to where he bought and sold stocks, he spent over an hour pouring over his investments making sure everything was earning him money. Before logging off, he checked on Flynn's so he could tell his brother he had.

After a long, cold shower, some coffee and a breakfast of oatmeal and fruit, he paced his living room wondering how early was too early to text, call or go see Norah. It wasn't even seven yet but he was dying to see her.

Those kisses from the night before had set him on fire. He hadn't had a make out session since early college but with Norah, it was enough. He liked being with her, laughing with her, hearing her talk or making sarcastic comments. The kissing with extra. Icing on the cake so to speak and sure, he was dying for more, but he could wait.

Grabbing his phone he turned it on to text her when he noticed he had a text from Flynn.

Flynn:

Joy says we are having you and apparently Norah over tonight. What's up with that?

Wyatt:

This is the first I heard about it.

Flynn:

So there's nothing going on with you and Norah?

Wyatt:

I didn't say that.

His phone rang. Of course it was Flynn.

"Did you really need to call me?"

"When my little brother has news that involves a woman, a call is warranted."

"There is no news."

"Don't bullshit me. It makes sense now because you were all moody when we were visiting mom and dad."

"Fuck you. I was not moody."

"Still moody I see."

Wyatt sighed into the phone. "Can you maybe not be an ass tonight."

"So there is something going on?"

"You're the one who said we were coming over. If Joy and Norah talked and they agreed, then I'll be there." Especially if Norah was willing to leave her apartment.

"You know when I see you together tonight I'm going to be able to tell if there is something going on."

"It's new okay and she's," how to describe her so his brother didn't terrify her, "reserved."

"Like I'm an ogre or something."

"If the shoe fits."

"I promise to be on my best behavior but you do know that if she's friends with Joy she is probably used to the way we are."

He'd never thought of that. And she really wasn't reserved. He'd just told Flynn that because of her situation. He had a feeling she was very used to people like Joy and could handle her with one hand tied behind her back.

"Just try not to embarrass her. She's...different."

"Wow. Okay. You really like this girl."

"Woman. She's a woman and yes I like her." More than liked her but he was barely able to admit that to himself let alone his brother.

"I promise to be on my best behavior."

"I'll believe it when I see it."

He hung up and quickly texted Norah

Wyatt:

I just heard that we are going to Joy and Flynn's tonight?

Norah:

Oh crap. Yeah I forgot to mention that she invited us over.

Wyatt:

And you are okay with this?

He waited but an answer never came. He was getting ready to text her again when a knock sounded on his door.

Pulling it open, he found Norah on the other side.

"I told Joy who I was," she rushed out as soon as the door was open.

He grabbed her hand, pulling her inside his apartment. "You did?"

"It felt right. She's been so good to me and I wanted her to know."

"That's why we're having this impromptu get together. Makes sense now."

"Is that okay?" She bit her lip making him groan inwardly. He wanted to be the one biting her lip.

"It's a great idea. I get to spend more time with you and you have the chance to get out a little. Win win."

Her eyes lit up and it was then that he finally took in what she was wearing. They looked like pajamas of some sort but they consisted of short shorts and a tank top that showed so much of her gorgeous skin.

And by the looks of it, she wasn't wearing a bra.

It was all he could do not to drool. Every time he'd seen her she'd been wearing baggy clothes that hung on her. This was different.

"Nice outfit."

She looked down at herself and immediately covered her chest with her arms. "Oh shit. I totally forgot that I wasn't dressed yet."

"Don't cover up on my account." He stepped closer making his intent known.

"Stay back," she lifted an arm, her hand touching his chest. "If you touch me right now, I will be useless all day and I have things I want to do."

He stopped moving his brow furrowing. "Well then you better go because if you stand here looking like that much longer, I might combust."

She laughed, her head dropping back. "You're a funny guy, Wyatt." She backed up. "So tonight, you're good to go with me?"

"Just try and stop me."

"Text me later and let me know what time you want to leave. I'll be ready." She turned to open the door. "Oh and Wyatt," her head whipped back around to face him, "this is already the best birthday I can remember." She left, leaving him staring after her wondering how he'd forgotten that it was her birthday. She'd told him but somehow it had slipped his mind.

Now that he remembered — or because she had mentioned it — he was going to make sure it really was the best one she'd ever had.

And for that, he needed help.

Lots and lots of help.

He started with Patrick. You couldn't have a birthday without cake and Dani made the best cake.

Wyatt:

I need a huge favor. Less from you and more from Dani.

It was early, so he wasn't sure if his friend would be up but he could wait if he wasn't. He didn't have to wait long though when a text came through.

Patrick:

What can I do for you?

Wyatt:

I need a cake. Today.

Patrick:

Are you trying to make Dani hate me?

Wyatt:

This is important. You know I wouldn't ask if it wasn't.

Patrick:

Give me the details. I can't promise anything but I'll ask Dani and let you know.

Wyatt:

I'll pay whatever it takes. Double her price.

Patrick:

Damn right you will.

He sent his friend all the info for the cake. He knew she liked chocolate because the other day when he'd brought her cupcakes from Dockside, she'd picked the chocolate ones first.

After that text, he sent one to Joy to let her know it was Norah's birthday and that he wanted to stop by early to decorate.

She agreed, telling him to go all out if he wanted.

And he definitely wanted.

Grabbing his coat, he set out to get things ready for what he hoped was going to be a great birthday for Norah.

He knocked on Norah's door a little before six. He'd texted her earlier to let her know what time he'd be by but as he sat in his apartment, he just couldn't wait any longer to see her.

When she opened the door, he was blown away by what he saw. She was wearing jeans that actually fit and a sweater that hugged her curves. For the first time, she even had on make-up.

His tongue was stuck to the top of his mouth.

"Hi," she said shyly.

He swallowed trying to find his voice. "You look..." he shook his head as words failed him.

"I hope that means I look better?"

"You could wear anything and you'd be beautiful but this new look shows off who you are a little more. And it puts a smile on your face. That's important."

"I do feel a little more like myself in these clothes."

"Did you go out to get them?"

She grabbed her coat off the table by the door. "No, I did the next best thing. I called Joy. She and I aren't the same size but she called around to her friends and found me a few pieces that worked."

He took her hand as she walked into the hallway. "I'll remember to thank her. But don't for one second think that the clothes make the woman. You need no help whatsoever getting my attention."

She stopped moving, her head looking up at him. "You always say the perfect thing."

He reached out, helping her slip her jacket on. "They aren't just words if that's what you're worried about. I mean everything I say."

"I should be jaded with everything that has happened to me. I should trust less and guard myself more, but I feel like..." she paused and shook her head. "I feel like I know myself. I know who to trust and who not to trust. Who's telling me the truth and who is just blowing smoke to get in my good graces. Brett is the one bad decision I've made in all my life and I can't let that...him get into my head."

He shook his head, marveling at her strength. "You blow me away." Leaning down, he lightly touched his lips to hers. He would have loved to do more, to devour her right there but that's not what she needed. And not what he needed.

He needed her to understand what he felt for her, how his heart beat fast and his brain got fuzzy, that had never happened to him before.

She'd made him feel more in four days than he'd ever felt before.

And shockingly, he wasn't scared of those feelings.

He wanted them.

And her.

She hesitated a little as they walked out the front door but he kept his hand on her lower back, guiding her towards his truck. He could feel her tension with being outside and wondered if this was how she'd felt every time she'd gone out.

He wanted to make her feel at ease.

"You met Joy right around the time she started dating my brother right?"

She nodded.

"Did she tell you the story about how Flynn carried her out of Avery's wedding?"

She looked up at him, her eyes wide. No more fear, only intrigue. "What? No, she never told me that."

"I wasn't there but from what I've heard, it was quite the scene. Everyone cheered them on mainly because Joy had been so steadfast in being with him."

She smiled and he felt the tension leave her body. "She was pretty adamant that he wasn't for her. It was pretty hilarious hearing her talk about him even after they were together."

"Flynn never wavered on her being the one. She was all he ever wanted from the moment he met her."

He opened the door to the truck and helped her inside. "That's sweet. And a little crazy."

"Tell me about it." He took one last look at her before closing the door and walking around to get inside.

Driving with her sitting right beside him, smelling amazing and looking even better was not easy. Before moving to Cedarville, he hadn't owned a car but once in town it was apparent he'd need one. The truck had been a hard sell. He'd wanted a small car but Flynn had convinced him that a truck was a better investment. Then one day, Joy had let it slip how easy it was to makeout in the truck compared to her car. He hadn't given it another thought until this moment. Now it was all he could think about.

Him and his dick.

It was a short drive to Flynn's house where he parked behind Dax's truck. He also spotted Brandon's truck and hoped that was all the guests for the night. He didn't want Norah to be overwhelmed.

"Wow this is a great house," she said as he put the car in park.

"Flynn built it. It took him a lot of years but he finally finished it last year."

"I can't wait to see the inside." She reached for the handle to get out but he put his hand on her knee to stop her.

"I'll come around." Quickly, he jumped out of the truck, striding around to the passenger side to open her door.

She didn't make a move to get out. Instead turned her head to look at him. "You know, the only other man who has ever opened a door for me was my dad."

"Then I'm in good company." He held his hand out for her to take. She eyed it for a second before finally reaching out to take it, letting him help her down.

"Do you know who all these cars belong to?" They walked toward the front of the house.

"The black one right there is Dax's so that means he and Avery are here and this one right here is Brandon's meaning that he and Leah are here."

She took a deep breath. "I can do this." She looked over at him. "Tell me I can do this?"

He lifted her chin with his fingers. "You can do this and if you can't, we'll leave. There is no pressure." He lowered his head, kissing her with the hope of calming her nerves.

"That helps," she said, her eyes still closed.

"Feel free to do it anytime you are feeling nervous."

She opened her eyes. "I might just do that."

They walked the rest of the way to the house, him giving her another second to pull herself together before they walked in.

He wanted this night to be perfect for her and if that meant giving her a few extra minutes here and there, he'd do it.

He'd pretty much do anything for her, he was finding out.

Chapter 8

With her hand in Wyatt's, she entered Joy and Flynn's home. She was more nervous than the day she'd hosted a two thousand dollar a plate fundraiser supporting child hunger. And that was saying something.

"You're here!" Avery shouted loudly, making her jump before embracing her in a hug. "Happy birthday!" Though they'd never met, it seemed natural to hug.

"Oh, thank you." She looked over Avery's shoulder to Wyatt who she assumed had spilled the beans. He shrugged with a smile on his face. When she stood back from Avery, it was then that she noticed all the decorations.

"Did you do this?" she asked Avery.

"Nope, this was all Wyatt."

There were streamers and balloons everywhere and even a sign saying happy birthday. It was...amazing.

"I'm overwhelmed."

She felt his fingers touch her elbow. " Birthdays are a big deal. You should get to celebrate."

Before she could respond more people came into the room.

"I'm mad at you," Joy said, not really looking mad. "How come you didn't tell me it was your birthday?"

"I guess it just slipped my mind." There was a giant of a man standing behind her.

"Ignore her," he said, "she's mad at everyone all the time." He stuck out his hand. "I'm Flynn."

"Nice to meet you, Flynn. You are exactly how Joy has described you."

He looked toward Joy. "I'm not sure I ever want to know how she describes me."

Joy shoved him. "Whatever, lumberjack."

"This is my husband, Dax," Avery said.

She shook his hand. "Nice to meet you." She looked at Flynn again. "Thank you for having us over tonight."

"That was all Joy. And whatever she wants, she gets."

Behind Dax was Brandon who waved hello and said, "And this is my soon to be wife, Leah."

The woman looked so familiar to Norah but she couldn't put her finger on why. "Happy birthday. I'm glad we could finally meet."

"This is all so nice of you guys to do." She was overwhelmed and badly wanted to retreat, but then Wyatt appeared at her side like he knew what she needed.

"Why don't we get a drink?"

She nodded and vaguely heard Joy telling them to help themselves.

"You looked like you needed a break," Wyatt said once they were out of earshot of everyone. The home was an open concept so it was just one gigantic room.

"It's crazy to me that you can notice that."

"I'm observant. Especially when it comes to you."

She looked around, finding a bottle of Pinot Noir on the counter and a wine glass. "Thank you for decorating. Last year I didn't get to celebrate and it was a hard day."

"I just want you to be happy."

"I am. Now." She took a sip of her wine. They were about to walk back to where everyone was when Leah joined them.

"Any chance I could talk to you for a quick second?" She was looking at her.

"Uh, sure."

Wyatt squeezed her hand before walking away.

"I look familiar to you right?" She paused. "What if I told you that my last name was Gibson?"

She stopped, glass of wine halfway to her mouth. Oh shit. Leah Gibson. They'd met. Years ago but they'd still met.

Norah had only been seventeen and she'd been in New York with her parents for a conference. One night while they'd been there, they went to dinner with a group of people and Leah had been there with her parents.

What a freaking coincidence.

"Don't freak. I'm not going to tell anyone who you are." She rested her hand on her arm in a reassuring gesture.

"Almost everyone here knows."

"They do?"

"Wyatt, Joy and Brandon."

"Brandon? My Brandon?" She put a hand to her chest and raised her eyebrows.

"He's a cop."

"Oh yeah, sometimes I forget that."

"He's only known since Monday."

"Are you okay?" She frowned. "I guess that's a stupid question. You are hiding or so it seems from a guy that can only be described as a crazy man who only wants you for your money and position and on top of that you had only recently lost your parents. Of course you're not okay."

Norah couldn't help but laugh at the way she summed up her life. "How is it that you can see him as a crazy man but the rest of the world doesn't?"

"I'm astute like that. Also, I've dealt with him in the past and when he hit on me, while engaged to you, I wanted to punch him. Almost did actually."

"Oh God, I would have paid to see that!"

"I'm sure some woman has punched him. He's too much of an ass to ignore that forever. Seriously though, I'm sorry he's put you in this situation. You have to know that you are safe here? Brandon would never let anything happen to you."

"I think I'm starting to see that this town protects their own. But that's not me. I'm an interloper."

"Bullshit. You chose this place for a reason and this town is special. Believe me, I know. When I ran from my former life, this is where I came and now, well I'm one of these crazy people."

"I think I'd like living here if I was actually living here. Pretty much all I do is hang out in my apartment."

"You're afraid someone will recognize you right? So you don't go out much?"

"That's it in a nutshell." She sipped her wine, wondering if her life was ever going to feel normal again.

"You shouldn't worry so much. One, I don't think Wyatt will ever leave your side." She raised her eyebrows. "That boy is already smitten. And two, you have friends now, and we will be on the lookout for anyone new or suspicious."

"I don't want to put anyone else in danger."

She didn't speak for a few seconds, the voices of the rest of the guests carrying into the kitchen. "I won't ask what you went through but I will tell you that you are strong for leaving."

She smiled. "That's what Wyatt keeps telling me."

"It's true," his voice interrupted them and when she turned, she found him standing behind her. "I take it Leah now knows?"

"We actually met once. Years ago," Leah said.

"I guess we should tell the rest of the party since it seems everyone here knows." She wasn't as apprehensive as she would have been days ago about telling people.

"We don't have to tell anyone else if you don't want others to know." Wyatt stepped in front of her, taking her hands in his. "This is your life and you can live it how you want."

She looked into his eyes and for the first time in a long while felt safe. "I think I'm ready to start living again."

They walked, hand-in-hand into the open living room where she quickly retold the story she had told several times that week. Avery and

Dax reacted the same way everyone else had but Flynn, he was hard to read.

"Flynn," Wyatt said, "you're quiet over there."

"You knew this?" He looked up to Joy who was sitting on the arm of the chair he was sitting in.

"I just found out the other day."

"Dammit, Joy, this could be dangerous."

"Flynn, it's not dangerous," Wyatt said.

He raised his arm, pointing at Wyatt. "I'll deal with you in a second. Joy, you can't not tell me things."

"It wasn't my story to tell and for that matter, I'm not some little woman who needs to be protected."

"I know that." He pulled her down onto his lap. "But I couldn't handle it if anything happened to you."

Norah watched as Joy softened. "It's the same with me but Flynn this doesn't concern me. And I really don't think Norah is in any danger."

"Brandon," Flynn said, "what do you think?"

He stood. "I'm inclined to lean toward Joy's opinion. There's no reason for me to suspect that Brett knows or suspects you are here. You covered your tracks well."

"Are you satisfied?" Wyatt's voice was stern making her wonder if that would be the voice he'd use during sex.

"You're my only brother, Wyatt and you haven't had the easiest year. I don't want you getting in over your head."

"Maybe I should go," she broke in before Wyatt could answer. She didn't want to cause an issue between brothers.

"No," Wyatt practically shouted. "Just ignore Flynn."

"I was about to say the same thing," Joy said. At his look she went on. "Babe I love you but you are being silly. She barely looks like the same person that she was in California and she is being careful. She's not out buying yachts and throwing parties. She never leaves her place, which is a secure building, might I add, and this town is safe."

"The two women who are standing in this room who were assaulted might have something to say about that."

Norah's mouth gaped open. "Who was assaulted?"

"Those were circumstantial situations," Leah said. "I had a guy who was pissed that my dad lost all his family's money, follow me here. He kidnapped me but I got away and all is well."

Norah had no idea how she talked so calmly about it.

"And I," Avery said, "had a man attack me at the car wash when he thought I was Joy."

"See right there," Flynn said. "He thought you were Joy."

"Because we're twins, you big dummy. Neither one of us will ever be mistaken for Norah. She's like three inches taller than us."

"You're missing the point on purpose, aren't you?"

"I think maybe Norah was right. We should leave."

"No." Joy shouted, standing. "Wyatt, you and Norah are staying. It's her birthday and she deserves to celebrate. Flynn, you are going to take Wyatt, go outside and deal with this. He's your brother and I hate seeing you fight. The rest of us are going to eat and enjoy the night." Hands on hips, she looked down to Flynn and then over to Wyatt. "Go. Now."

"Your sister is a badass," Dax said to Avery when Flynn and Wyatt were gone.

"And don't you forget it," Joy said, lifting her beer and downing the whole thing.

"Who's hungry?" Leah said. "We have tons of food and I for one need to eat before I drink anymore."

Avery walked over to her, guiding her to the kitchen. "Don't worry. They will be fine. I don't know how much you know about Wyatt and the year he's had but it wasn't great. Flynn is just worried."

"Wyatt told me all about his year and I don't want to add anymore stress to him."

"I don't think you are stressing him out. On the contrary. I think he is relaxed and happy since he met you. I don't know him well but Joy does and she told me how unhappy he was when he moved here. I think you might be good for him."

"I don't know what we're even doing. We just met." She was confused about a lot of things but what she felt for Wyatt in a short amount of time was not one of them.

"Do me a favor okay, and don't let time be a deciding factor in whether you let yourself like him. Hearts don't work on a timeline. And I should know. I think I loved Dax after our first date."

"Really?" That was crazy to Norah. She had taken months to even decide if she liked Brett. Admittedly, she was smart to do so knowing what she knew about him now.

"Yep and he," she smiled, the happiness going all the way to her eyes, "well, he would probably tell you that he fell in love the first time he saw me."

"That's incredible."

"If you ask me, it happens more than you think."

Norah thought about that as she filled her plate with food. She'd never been one to listen to her heart when it came to love. She liked to take her time, make sure things fit. Look how that worked out for her. Not great. But was falling for someone so easily, so quickly any better? Was there any substance to a relationship that started so fast?

Looking over to Dax and Avery, she decided that last part was stupid. Of course there was. Dax was nuzzling her neck, or trying to as she filled a plate full of food. She kept giggling and swatting his hand when he stole food from the plate.

Then there was Leah and Brandon. Leah was whispering something to him and Brandon was stroking his hand down her back. Their love was evident.

She was lost in her own thoughts, when she felt a hand touch her back. Looking to the side, she found Wyatt right next to her.

He was so handsome that her mouth dried up and she couldn't speak.

"Sorry about that. I just had to explain things to Flynn." He took the plate from her hands and kept filling it up. "He was just worried that I was in over my head." He stopped in front of the drinks. "I told him I might be," he looked over to her, "but that I liked how it felt and wanted to try."

"And what did he say to that?" She filled her wine glass and grabbed him a beer.

"That he understood because he'd felt the same way about Joy. He just didn't want me to get hurt." He touched her elbow with his free hand. "You're not going to hurt me are you?"

She laughed because really, what else could she do in that situation. "I have no fucking clue."

He joined in with her laughter. "That's good enough for me."

They found seats in the living room, him sitting right next to her and sharing the plate of food like they'd been doing it for years.

"I ran into Addison in town today," Leah said, "and I swear to God she is bigger than when I saw her last week."

"And miserable," Avery said. "She came into work with Ryan the last two days because I guess Tony told her to take her leave early so she could have some time to relax and man did that piss her off. So instead of working she came in with Ryan who, I swear must love her so much because he didn't once get annoyed or pissy with her. I, on the other hand, wanted to murder her."

"How is it that she is all grumpy but Carly is nicer than she's ever been?" Joy asked. "I kinda want her to be pregnant forever."

"You and me both," Brandon said seriously.

Wyatt leaned in close, whispering in her ear. "Carly is Brandon's cousin. She is married to Tony who is Addison's brother. Both Addison and Carly are pregnant."

"I think I got that last part." She wanted him to keep whispering in her ear. It felt so good having his breath on her skin.

"Oh sorry," Leah said. "I forgot that you don't know everyone."

She waved her hand in front of her face. "It's no problem. Joy has talked about most of them so I've kinda figured some of it out."

"Well, if you ever meet Addison and Carly just know that right now we are in bizarro world." Joy rolled her eyes. "Once those babies come, maybe they'll go back to normal."

"She's not kidding," Dax added. "It's like Freaky Friday all of a sudden."

Avery patted him on the back. "Nice movie reference, honey." She explained. "Until Dax and I started dating, I swear he hadn't seen a movie since high school. He was useless with pop culture references."

"I think Wyatt was like that for the last few years," Flynn said. "He was so absorbed in work that I don't think he watched a movie that whole time."

"I've since caught up." He shrugged. "Being a building owner has a lot of down time."

"I watch a lot of TV and movies," Norah said. "It's one of the only things I have to do since I barely leave my apartment."

"I think that's about to change," Flynn said. "Or at least you won't be alone watching those movies."

She looked to her side, taking in Wyatt's handsome smile. "I like the thought of having company."

Chapter 9

Sitting in his car next to Norah, Wyatt kept his eyes on the road as he drove. To him, their night out with his friends had been one of the best in his life. He'd gotten to sit next to her for hours and enjoy her company.

That was better than anything he'd ever done before.

Until now.

He liked being alone with her, listening to her talk and ramble on.

When he'd first met her, he'd assumed she was shy. Turns out, that was just because of her circumstances. She was the least shy person he'd met.

She was telling him the story of the time she'd met Leah and her words were coming out a mile a minute.

"I'm still amazed that she lives here in Cedarville and just so happens to be one of the people in your group of friends."

"It's a small town." He shrugged hoping his short answer would keep her talking. He loved listening to her.

"I don't know how I'm going to go back to being a hermit after tonight. I had so much fun."

"You don't have to, you know. None of us would ever let anything happen to you. Especially me."

She leaned her head back on the seat and turned it to look at him. "Why is that? I mean, I know why you moved here and all you've been through but why is there not a woman in your life?"

He looked over to her, then back at the road. "When I moved here I was a mess." At her look of doubt he went on. "Seriously, I was. I'd lost weight, looked pale and sick. It took weeks to feel normal again. Dating or even being out in public was not high on my list. Flynn was the only person I saw for days at a time and only because he forced himself into my life. After a while, I finally started to feel like my old self again. The one from before New York. But I still felt like an outsider here.

Eventually, Flynn and Joy made me start going with them to events and just like that, I had friends. I thought about dating but I didn't want to complicate my life too soon." He looked at her again. "Then I met you and that all went out the window."

"I know what it's like to lose yourself somewhere along the way. Honestly, I still feel a little lost. I want to be the person I was before, the person who was strong and happy. And I'm trying. It's just scary thinking that one day I might be out and Brett might find me."

"I won't ever let him hurt you."

"I know you think that but you can't be with me all the time. You have a life."

"If you haven't noticed, my life is pretty open. Managing the buildings doesn't take up a whole lot of my time. So when you say I can't be with you all the time, I wholeheartedly disagree." He wondered for a second if she even wanted that. "Unless you don't want me with you?"

"No," she was quick to reply, her hand landing on her arm, "I like the thought of being with you but I don't want you to change your life for me."

"In case you haven't noticed, my life is pretty boring. Hanging out with you will add some much needed spice to my life."

She laughed, shaking her head. "I'm not sure what I did in this world to deserve your undivided attention but I'm not going to question it. Being with you feels good."

He looked over to her again. "It's settled. If you want to go somewhere, come to me first and I'll make myself available to escort you."

Pulling into the lot at the apartment complex, he shut off the truck and turned to face her. "I'm not ready for this night to end."

Her palm slid down his arm until her fingers entwined with his. "Me either."

Seconds ticked by with neither of them moving. Finally, he opened his door, begrudgingly letting go of her hand. Before she could get out of the truck herself, he ran around the front to open her door for her.

"Thank you." She took his offered hand and stepped down, her body facing his. "Your mom really did raise you right didn't she?"

"This was actually my dad. He said that any man who doesn't open the door for a woman is a piece of shit. His exact words."

"Sounds a little like my dad." They started to walk. "When I started dating, the guys had to come to the door to get me and if they didn't my dad wouldn't let me leave the house."

"If I had ever done that, well, I'm not sure what my dad would have done."

In the entryway, between their two apartments, they stopped. "Any chance you'd want to hang at your place?" she asked. "I've spent a lot of time inside mine the last year so getting away is a treat."

"My place it is." He unlocked and opened the door, allowing her to go in ahead of him. "Plus, here I have cookies that my mom made and sent home with me."

"You expect me to eat cookies after I ate two pieces of that fantastic cake? You are an evil man, Wyatt Murray."

"There's no pressure to eat the cookies. But they are double chocolate fudge." He raised his eyebrows at her.

"Like I said, evil."

He laughed as he switched on a few lights. "Something to drink?"

"I wouldn't say no to a beer."

He moved into the kitchen and grabbed two bottles out of his fridge. After opening them both, he handed her one. He picked up the container of cookies and carried them into the living room.

"Seriously, I don't think I can eat a cookie."

"There's no pressure." He opened the container and snatched one for himself. His mom really did make the best cookies.

"I have no idea how you can still be hungry." She fake rolled her eyes and because he was obviously a sick man, he got hard.

Dropping the cookie back in the container, he warned, "Tell me know if you don't want this?" He was on edge and needed her in his arms.

She laughed. "What do you think I'm doing here, Wyatt." She gripped the front of his shirt, closing the distance between them. "Kiss me now."

He didn't hesitate. Why would he when they seemed to be on the same page. Her lips were soft under his, moving in perfect sync with his own. His hands found their way to her hips, his fingers digging in through her jeans. The moan she let out spurred him on even more. And when she pushed him backward and climbed on top of him, he thanked God that he'd moved to this small town and bought this building.

"I'm dying here, Wyatt," she said when he trailed his lips down her neck.

"You and me both." His words were muffled against her skin. His hands were moving up and down her back until they finally settled on her ass.

Having her on top of him, her body molded to his, was torture. The best kind of torture. Only one thing would make it better.

Her naked.

His cock was hard between them and there was no way she couldn't feel him.

She started grinding her body against his, making his cock swell even more. He wasn't going to last. If she kept it up, he knew without a doubt that he would come in his pants.

And how embarrassing would that be.

Thankfully, she sat up. He thought maybe they were finished or in what would be a glimmer of hope, she wanted to go to his bedroom. But neither happened.

Instead, she moved down the couch, her hand brushing over his cock as she did so.

"I don't want to be too forward, but," she bit her lip, "take off your pants."

He was shocked at her candor, making him raise an eyebrow. "What about you?"

"We'll get to me but first I am going to do something that I have pretty much been thinking about since I met you."

He started to unhook his belt. "And what is that?"

"I'm going to give you the greatest blowjob you've ever had."

Her words stopped him in his tracks and honestly he almost had a heart attack. "W-what?"

She began to help him remove his belt. "You don't know this about me, but I love doing this. Love it. Like it makes me so hot." She had his belt off and began working on his button and zipper. "And doing it to you, for you, well let's just say that I have been in a perpetual state of arousal for days."

He swallowed the lump that had formed in his throat. He couldn't speak, couldn't even form words.

She leaned forward over him, her face close to his. "I promise you, I am not doing anything that I don't want to be doing."

Those words put him into action. At the speed of light, he shed his pants leaving him in his boxers. Because it felt odd to have on his boxers with his shirt, he pulled that off too.

She ran her hand down his torso. "Later, I'd like to spend some time admiring your chest, but right now, I have plans." Her palm gripped him through his boxers and he hissed out a breath. "This seems pretty impressive. Maybe I should get a better look." Eyes on his, she lowered his boxers down his legs. When they were off, she finally broke eye contact and looked down.

"Fuck." She continued to stare at his cock. When she finally looked up, she winked and said, "This is going to be fun," and then finally, touched him with her hand.

It felt so good to have her skin touch his bare cock. He was so pent up that there was no way he was going to last but damn if he didn't care. He had a feeling she would definitely be in favor of doing this more than once.

He wanted to close his eyes and relish in how good it felt to have her hand moving up and down his cock but he was glad he didn't when he watched her lower her head down and take him into her mouth.

Warm, wet and wonderful was all he could think.

She moved over him with the precision of a person who loved giving head. He couldn't remember another time in his life where he'd felt that the woman actually enjoyed it. But Norah, she sucked his dick with gusto.

And man did he wish he could last forever.

Her mouth moved up and down and every so often she'd swirl her tongue at the top. She'd only gone about three quarters of the way down his length which was fine by him but when she bottomed out and he felt her swallow him into the back of her throat, he was done for.

He came with a shout not at all caring if anyone in the building could hear.

She sat back, a satisfied look on her face. "God I love doing that."

He laughed and pulled her down on top of him. "I'm willing anytime you feel the desire."

"It doesn't bother you that I like doing that?"

Tilting his head, he looked at her. "Why would it bother me?"

"Someone once told me that because I loved doing it I was a whore."

"Let me guess, Brett told you that?"

She nodded. "I know he's not someone I should listen to but it still stuck with me."

"There's nothing wrong with liking anything sexual. If you and your partner are in agreement, nothing is dirty or whorish."

"He never let me do it."

That made him sad and happy at the same time. He didn't want to think of her doing what she'd just done with anyone else let alone that asshole. But he also hated that he'd made her feel dirty for something she enjoyed.

"You are free to do that anytime you want. With me."

"I will probably take you up on that."

He sat up, taking her with him. "Now that you've had your fun, I think it's my turn."

"What did you have in mind?"

He stood, still naked, taking her with him. "You'll find out in about five minutes." Taking a few steps, he turned and looked at her. "You coming?"

"Oh hell yeah."

Her smile was huge as she walked beside him to his bedroom. Thanks to her blowjob his pent up sexual frustration was gone. Now though, all he could think about was tasting her and pleasing her. He wanted her to have the same out of body experience that she'd given him.

He'd never had any complaints but he'd also never had anyone tell him that he was a master pussy licker.

There was a chance he was horrible.

As soon as they were in his room, she began to undress which was only fair since he was naked. He watched with admiration as she stripped off her jeans then pulled her sweater over her head. In only a bra and panties, she stood in front of him.

Beautiful.

It was the only word to describe the way she looked.

"You're gorgeous."

She reached out her hand to him, drawing him closer. "You make me feel gorgeous."

He kissed her lips, lingering for several moments. His fingers ran up and down her sides, her skin pebbling at his touch. Deepening the kiss, he easily worked to remove her bra and then slowly lowered her to his bed.

Getting his first look at her bare breasts, he watched as they moved with her heavy breathing. Big, firm and round, each one was begging for his mouth.

Lowering his head, he took one tight nipple into his mouth, twirling his tongue around the tip. She moaned under him, pushing herself further into his mouth. With his other hand, he cupped the other breast, teasing the nipple with his fingers. Her skin tasted fresh, like she'd just showered even though he knew she hadn't.

Needing more, he kissed down her body, lingering as much as he could on each patch of skin. Ribs, stomach, hips and then finally he was settled between her legs. Her underwear was damp with her arousal making his cock swell again. He ran a finger down her covered center and had the pleasure of hearing her moan his name.

He would never get sick of his name coming from her mouth.

Stripping her panties down her legs, he dipped one finger barely inside. Feeling her wetness and her grip sent him over the edge. He dove face first into her pussy, licking and sucking with abandon. She tasted like the sweetest honey he'd ever had and he couldn't get enough.

He heard her incoherent words from above him and kept going. He'd wanted to do this all day. When he added a finger to pump inside her, he felt her shake and then go over the edge. Her release went on and on and because he was already addicted to her, he didn't stop. He loved how she tasted on his tongue and loved how she writhed under him.

He was pretty sure he just loved her.

Which was insane.

But made him feel so good inside.

When her second orgasm pulsed through her body, he finally came up for air, smiling and covered in her juices.

"Are you trying to kill me?" She had a look of satisfaction on her face and she was breathing heavily.

"I would never want to do that. Just enjoying myself." He dropped down next to her on the bed, pulling her into his side.

"I'm glad you enjoyed yourself because it felt amazing."

"'I know something else that could feel amazing." He raised his eyebrows hoping she understood what he was talking about.

Laughing she rolled until she was on top of him. "Yeah, anything I might know about?"

"I guess we can see and find out." His lips found hers and they kissed heavily until they were both panting. Needing to be inside her, he reached under his pillow for the condom he'd stashed there that morning just in case.

As he started to open it, she snatched it from his hand and ripped it open. Scooting back, she slid it down his cock with the speed of light and then before he knew it, had him lined up with her opening. All he had to do was push and he'd be inside her.

One push.

And he'd be in heaven.

It was scary and crazy to think like that but it was how he felt.

Gripping her hips, he pushed up at the same time as she lowered down and in one motion he was fully seated inside of her.

"Holy shit," she moaned.

"You feel so good," he told her as she started to move.

Up and down she went adding hip swivels here and there. With her on top, he had the pleasure of watching her tits bounce in his face. Reaching up, he cupped them both in his large hands, levered himself up, and took one in his mouth. Her moans of approval and pleasure filled his ears as they moved in sync. Needing more, he gripped her ass and flipped them over so that she was beneath him.

Her eyes bore into his as he furiously pumped into her. Her hands were on his ass like she was afraid he was going to stop.

There was no chance of that.

He'd do this forever with her if he could.

When she tensed with her release he let himself relax and let go. It was possibly the best feeling he'd ever had.

Not wanting to but knowing he needed to pull out, he rolled to the side. After dealing with the condom, he pulled her into his side, loving how easily she went.

"I forgot how much I love sex."

"I'm not sure I've ever had sex like that. If I had, I'd never have been able to stop."

She was playing with his hair. "Yeah, you might be right. It's never been that...easy nor has it ever felt so...right."

"For a minute I was worried it was just me."

She smiled. "Nope, it was definitely not just you."

"I can't believe you've been here, right under my nose for months and I never met you."

"I can't believe I never came up with an excuse to get you into my apartment after the first time I saw you."

He stared at her trying to figure out what to say next. He wanted to tell her how he felt, that as far as he was concerned, she was it for him. But he couldn't. Not yet.

When she yawned, he pulled the covers up over them. "We should get some sleep. It's been a long day."

"You're okay with me sleeping here?"

"Did you want to leave?"

"No, but I wasn't sure you'd want me to."

He leaned over and flipped the lamp off. "I will always want you here."

"Thank you. For making me feel safe. For making this the best birthday ever and for just being you. This was the best day I've ever had."

"You humble me, Norah. Sleep, there will be time tomorrow for everything else."

Chapter 10

Waking up in the arms of a man after almost two years of sleeping alone should have felt odd. But with Wyatt, it felt totally normal. More than normal. It felt right. She wasn't sure if this was normal or not though. With Brett, it had taken months to feel normal and even then it never felt like this moment.

Although to be fair she probably shouldn't use Brett as an example.

Wyatt's arms tightened around her — it still shocked her that she'd slept in his arms the whole night — and he murmured in her ear.

"Go back to sleep."

"Why should I when we are both awake." She turned in his arms to face him. His hair was a mess, sticking out in all directions and his smoothe face now held a little day or two of facial hair.

"Hi," he said sleepily. "How'd you sleep?"

"Really well. You?"

"Better than I have in forever."

"You are fantastic for my ego, you know that?" She'd never been with anyone who complimented as much as Wyatt.

"I speak the truth." He reached out with his arm and pushed hair off her face. "Wanna spend the day with me?"

"What did you have in mind?"

"I was thinking we could go see a movie. If you wanted?"

"Yes I want." She hadn't seen a movie in an actual theater in so long and it was something she loved to do.

"Maybe before we do that, we can..." he trailed off as he rolled on top of her.

"You have the best ideas." She met him halfway for a kiss that turned hot in only seconds.

Without hardly a break, he'd donned a condom and slipped inside her with ease. Their lovemaking was slow and sensual, unlike the night before when it was hurried and wild. The difference was astounding and she couldn't decide which one she enjoyed more.

After, as they lounged in his bed, still breathing heavily, she wondered if it was always going to be like this. Would the sex always be so all consuming?

"I have a feeling it will be."

"Huh?"

"You asked if it was always going to be like this?"

Oh hell. "I said that out loud?" Sex apparently fried her brain.

He laughed. "Yeah, you did."

She closed her eyes and chastised herself for being so stupid.

"Don't be embarrassed. I was wondering something similar."

She turned her head to look at him. "You were?"

"How could I not when I've never felt anything like this before."

She sighed. This man was from another world. There were guys who said stuff just to get the girl but with Wyatt, she knew, somehow, that what he was saying was from his heart. He would never just say words to get a girl into bed.

Hell, she was already in his bed. She'd needed no coaxing.

"If I don't get out of this bed right now," she said as she sat up, "we are never going to leave this apartment."

"Fine by me." He crossed his arms under his head, seemingly happy to just stay there all day.

Standing, she picked up her pillow, throwing it at him. "Get up, goofball."

She went in search of her clothing, which was strewn about his room. After she'd found it all, she looked up to find him still on his bed, watching her.

"I'm gonna go home and shower. Wanna meet in an hour?" That would give her enough time to get ready and have breakfast.

Moving fast, he stood and pulled on a pair of shorts he picked up from the floor. "I'd like it better if you showered here but that's my heart speaking. My head knows that all the stuff you need is next door."

"I'll only be gone an hour." She smiled, unable to stop herself.

"I'll walk you over."

"You don't have to." Although him wanting to made her heart flip in her chest.

"I do have to. I promised to be with you and this is one of those times."

She faced him, her hand coming up to caress his naked chest. "Thank you."

He gripped the wrist of the hand that was touching him. "No thanks necessary." He moved in closer, his lips dropping down on hers. "Consider me yours to use anyway you see fit."

"I'll remember that later."

He walked her to her door, waiting until she was inside with the door locked before he walked away. She knew that because she watched him through the peephole.

Needing a moment, she flopped down onto her couch and closed her eyes. Wyatt made her feel so good. After all she'd been through she honestly had never thought she'd find a man like him again.

She never thought she'd have a life outside this damn apartment.

Now she had friends and she had Wyatt. Who she guessed was her boyfriend. It was surreal to her that in the blink of an eye her life had changed. Although if she thought about it, that was how it had changed before. Even though that was a bad change.

If it could happen once it could happen a second time.

And the sex. It was beyond anything she'd ever known. He cared and spent time making sure she was happy. That had not been something she'd ever experienced.

She felt as if she was living in a fairy tale. Only she'd never believed in fairy tales.

Until now.

Wyatt was definitely her prince charming.

Letting out a breath, she stood up. The sooner she was showered and ready, the sooner she could see Wyatt again.

During her shower it hit her that she was sore. Sore in places that she might have never been sore in. That right there told her that sex before Wyatt hadn't been special.

Just basic.

And now that she'd had the good kind of sex, she wasn't planning on going back.

Showered, dressed and drinking coffee, she heard a knock on her door at the same time her phone dinged with a text.

Wyatt:

Knock knock.

Laughing at his double entrance, she unlocked the door, opening it to him.

"That was the longest hour of my life." He stepped into her apartment, shutting the door behind him. He had her in his arms, lips on hers within seconds.

"I'm pretty sure it wasn't even an hour." His lips were tenderly kissing her neck, his facial hair tickling her skin.

"Forty-eight minutes," he said against her skin. "Way too long."

She pushed him away. "You stay over there." Heat pooled between her legs and she wanted nothing else but to throw caution to the wind and stay in her apartment all day.

But there was time for that later.

She noticed that he was holding a wrapped package in his hand. "What's that?"

"This?" He held it out in front of him. "Oh it's nothing. Just a birthday gift for someone special."

She swallowed, looking up at him. "You got me a birthday gift?"

"You sound surprised?"

"Why didn't you give it to me last night?"

He looked shy as he shrugged. "I wanted to do it in private and then by the time we got home...well we were otherwise occupied." He held it out for her to take. "Happy birthday."

She took the gift and moved to her couch to sit down. He followed her, sitting down right next to her. "You didn't have to get me anything at all."

"I wanted you to have a good memory of this birthday."

She stopped opening the present, looking at him. "I already had the best birthday. This is just extra."

"Go ahead, open it."

She finished unwrapping the package, pulling off the lid to the box. Inside wrapped in tissue paper was a framed picture of her with her mom and dad that had been taken at one of her Eversware software launch parties.

"When I was visiting my parents, I found this online and thought how perfect it was for you. I noticed that you didn't have any pictures of your family and thought maybe I could rectify that."

She was speechless. It was possibly the best gift anyone had ever given her. As she looked at how happy the three of them had been in the picture, she felt a tear slid down her cheek.

"You are the most amazing man." Her voice was rough as she tried to hold back more tears.

"I didn't mean to make you cry." He reached out, taking her hand in his. "I thought this would make you happy."

"It does make me happy. More than you will ever know." She sat the frame down on the coffee table and wrapped her arms around his neck. "Thank you, Wyatt. Thank you so much."

"You're more than welcome." He hugged her back, his arms feeling so good around her back.

"I wasn't sure this day could get any better," she said when she pulled back, "but I should have known you'd find a way to out do even yourself."

"I aim to please."

"Should we look to see what movies are playing?"

"Sure." He pulled out his phone and clicked on a movie app. They browsed through together finally deciding on an action adventure flick. The theater was not in town though. It was in the next town over, Woodridge. That scared her a little being that it was a larger town, but she pushed down her fear with the knowledge that she got to spend the day with Wyatt.

Sitting in a movie theater for the first time in almost two years was a treat. Doing it next to Wyatt was incredible. He held her hand, stroked her thigh and even kissed her neck once or twice.

It was like she was back in high school on a first date.

Only this time, she knew how the date would end.

After the movie, they drove back into Cedarville for a late lunch at Dockside. The place was packed so they had to wait at the bar for a few minutes for a table.

"Wes has really done a great job with this place," he told her. "It opened a couple of months after I moved to town and since then, it's been the place to go."

"It's busy." That part she didn't love.

"Oh hell, is it too much?" he asked, concern in his voice. "We can leave?"

She touched his arm. "No I'm okay, especially with you by my side." It was true even if she still had a little bit of anxiety about the crowd.

They moved closer to the bar when two women walked away. "What can I get ya?" A woman asked.

"Hey, Sabrina, meet Norah." He introduced her to the bartender and they shook hands.

"Nice to meet you," Sabrina said. "Joy has mentioned you a few times."

"Thank you."

"What can I get you guys?"

"I'll have a MadTree," she spook up first and Wyatt said he'd have the same.

Sabrina walked away to grab their drinks and she turned toward Wyatt. "Maybe we can go by Joy's salon? I'd like to see the other building you own."

"We can. I warn you, it's not much. Pretty small."

"It's still pretty cool that you own a couple of buildings."

"I'm not in Logan's league but I think I am doing all right."

"Logan is Brandon's brother right? Married to Melanie?"

"That's him."

"How many buildings does he own?"

"From what I know, he owns the whole side of the strip that his gallery is in. You'll see it when we go to Joy's."

"I think I've walked by it when I went to the grocery store."

"How often do you shop?"

"I do a big trip once a month and try to go every two weeks for fresh stuff. Sometimes I get so nervous at the thought of leaving though that I just do without."

He leaned in close, his breath caressing her cheek. "I will bring you fresh fruit or vegetables every day if you want."

She stroked his cheek. "That just means I'll have to eat healthy."

"I can counter that with burgers and fries from here." He winked as he grabbed their beers from the counter, holding one out for her to take.

"Julia is in the back," Sabrina said. "Actually so is Dani." She shook her head. "Those two always seem to be here."

Norah looked up to Wyatt for clarification. "Julia is Wes's wife and is a therapist when she's not here helping out. Dani is Patrick's girlfriend. She is the one who makes the amazing cupcakes and who made your cake last night." He took her hand in his. "Would you like to go back and meet them?"

Nervousness took over her body but she pushed it down. "If you think that would be cool."

"I'm positive it will be fine." They walked hand in hand each carrying their beer in the opposite hand. Wyatt pushed through the door that separated the dining area from the kitchen.

"Hey, Wyatt." A gorgeous, curvy woman greeted him.

"Hi, Julia." He never let her hand go as he pulled her to stand next to him. "This is Norah."

"Hi, Norah," the woman who he'd called Julia said. "Joy has mentioned you a few times. It's nice to finally meet you."

"And this is Dani," Wyatt said. "The creator of your cake and all those cupcakes you love."

"Hi," Dani said. "I hope you liked the cake."

"I loved the cake. You are a genius with icing."

"I can attest to that," a man who had been cooking said. "I'm Patrick and her icing is my favorite thing in this world."

Dani slapped him. "You said it like that on purpose so it would sound dirty."

Patrick shrugged. "If you thought it sounded dirty maybe it's because you have a dirty mind."

"You both have dirty minds," the other man said. "It's like a frat house in here when you're together."

"And this is Wes," Wyatt said. "He's the master of the burger and fries you love so much."

"It's nice to meet you. I hope we aren't bothering you."

"Not at all," Julia said. "What are you guys out doing today?"

"We saw a movie and now we're grabbing a late lunch," Wyatt answered.

Patrick looked between them. "Oh I see now, this is the elusive woman who you bought take out for the other day."

This time Julia was the one who slapped his arm. "Seriously, Patrick. You don't just go saying things like that."

"What? I didn't say anything bad."

Norah was laughing. No wonder people loved this town. The residents were quite funny.

"I'd apologize for him," Dani said, "but honestly, it wouldn't help. He tends to say what's on his mind."

"It's fine," she said, still laughing, "I'm getting used to the people around here just saying whatever they think."

"We're having a girls night tomorrow at Carly's," Julia said, "you should come."

"Oh," she looked at Wyatt. "I wouldn't want to impose." She also wasn't sure if she could go and feel comfortable.

"Nonsense," Julia said. "Carly won't care. Plus Dani is making dessert so you can't miss it."

"Can I think about it and let you know?" She wanted to go but she also wanted to know that she felt safe.

"Sure." Julia handed her a card. Here's my number. Call or text and let me know. And I will tell Carly I invited you so she is aware."

She and Wyatt went back out to the restaurant where their table was ready.

"I think you should go," he said as they sat. "You already know most everyone there and it would be good for you."

"I want to go. I'm just nervous."

"About what?"

She pursed her lips. "Everything. That Brett will find me or that people will think I'm a freak or even that they won't like me. Everything about being out in public scares me."

He reached across the table, taking her hand. "I understand that and I, more than anyone, want you to feel safe. What if I made you a deal? I will take you there and then I will pick you up. You won't have to walk outside alone at all."

"That takes care of the being afraid Brett will find me part but it does nothing about my irrational fear that the rest of the group won't like me."

"Half of them have already met you and they like you. Also, I don't think Joy will let anyone not like you. She's a force to be reckoned with."

She laughed, rolling her eyes. "You make good points."

"You can do this, I know you can and while I'll miss you, I think you need to start remembering who you were before you came here."

She swallowed and squeezed his hand. "I'll go." Inside she felt like she'd just taken a huge step.

A leap of faith.

But really, what did she have to lose?

Chapter 11

Sitting in his truck, Wyatt wondered if he'd done the right thing by pushing Norah into going to Carly's house.

He'd dropped her off fifteen minutes ago but still he sat outside in his truck in the driveway. He was finding it hard to make himself leave.

Maybe he should have made plans himself. Something to keep his mind off Norah.

The second he had that thought, a loud knock sounded against his window.

It was Flynn.

Rolling it down, he said, "What the hell, man."

"I could say the same thing to you. What are you doing sitting here?"

"I dropped Norah off."

"You dropped her off fifteen minutes ago and I know this because Joy texted me and told me."

"So you what, came back to check up on me?" That was his brother, always looking out for him.

"Come on, let's get out of here. I'll drive."

After rolling up the window, he got out of his truck and into Flynn's.

"I can't believe she told you I was out here." Joy was the best, but she sure was a pain in his ass sometimes.

"She cares about you."

Softening he said, "And I care about her. You couldn't have picked anyone better."

"You think I picked her? The fucking universe picked her. I had nothing to do with it. She was mine the second I saw her." He looked over toward him. "And I'm gonna go ahead and guess that's how it was for you with Norah."

He nodded unsure if he could get the words out about just how much she already meant to him. "Do you think that's normal? Falling that fast?"

"Normal is overrated. When you know you know and not acting on it doesn't make it magically go away. "

Wyatt eyed him speculatively. "Have you always been this wise?"

He scoffed. "Damn right I have."

They laughed and then changed the subject to their mom until they pulled up to Dockside. Inside they found Tony, Logan, Ryan and Dax.

"Look who I picked up along the way," Flynn said as they pulled up chairs. "He was parked outside the house like a freaking guard dog."

"Hey I would have been inside the house watching over my very pregnant wife if she'd have allowed it," Tony said.

"I tried too," Ryan added. "Addison wouldn't even let me drop her off, saying that she couldn't drink but she could drive."

Flynn looked at him. "Looks like you aren't the only one who didn't want to go."

Wyatt punched his brother in the arm. "This coming from the man who follows Joy around like a puppy."

"Fuck off."

"You first."

"Boys," Dax said. "No need to fight."

"Okay, dad," Flynn said, earning him a middle finger from Dax.

"Hey I like when my girl goes out with the ladies," Logan said. "She comes home drunk and damn if the sex with a drunk Melanie isn't off the chains."

"Or maybe it's in chains," Tony said, raising his eyebrows.

Wyatt was laughing as he ordered a beer. These were the things he'd missed out on when he'd lived in New York and was working twenty hour days. He never had any real friends. And even though these guys were new friends, he knew for a fact that he could call any one of them up and they'd help out if and when needed.

"Tony, I hear you are hiring another employee?" Ryan said.

"Yeah, with Addison taking maternity leave and then only planning to work part time for a few years, I'm gonna need the help."

"Have you found anyone yet?" Logan asked.

"I think I have. He applied online and while he doesn't currently live around here, he's willing to relocate."

"That's great news," Ryan said. "I know how bad Addison feels about leaving you in the lurch."

"She'd doing no such thing. I am happy to take the backseat to my niece or nephew."

As Wyatt listened to them all talk about their lives, he couldn't help but think of what his own future might hold. All the images held Norah.

He wanted her for a lifetime. Longer if possible.

Wes approached their table. "Settle down out here."

"Hey!" Dax yelled. "It's my brother!"

Wes scrutinized Dax. "You say that like you never see me even though you just saw me this morning."

"I know but I just like having you around."

"Well I only have a second but I have some news and figured since you are all here, this was as good a time as any to spill the beans."

"Better be good news," Flynn said.

"The best news. Julia is pregnant."

Cheers went up all around.

"That's fantastic news!" Tony said, standing to congratulate Wes.

"I'm gonna be an uncle," Dax said, hugging his brother. "This really is the best news."

Wyatt stood along with everyone else and gave his congratulations to Wes.

"Congrats, man."

"Thanks everyone. Julia is a little freaked out due to her age but we are going to listen to the doctor and do whatever she says."

"Everything will be fine," Logan said.

"I've gotta get back but you guys have fun." Wes walked away as silence settled around the table.

"Wow," Ryan said, "seems like there will be a lot of babies soon."

Flynn looked at Dax. "I thought for sure you and Avery would be next."

"Believe me, we're trying. But I thought it would be Logan and Mel." He looked at Logan. "What's the hold up?"

"Mel wants to wait just a little bit, which is fine by me."

"What about you, Flynn?"

His brother laughed. "I think I'd like to be married first."

"That's happening soon," Tony said.

"A lot of quick engagements in this town," Logan said.

"I was thinking the same thing," Wyatt said.

"Says the man who was mooning outside the house his girlfriend was at. I don't think you get a say so."

"If it's what you want, don't wait. Life is fucking short." Logan saluted him with his beer.

Flynn rubbed his beard. "You do already have the ring."

"What? No I don't?" Wyatt was shocked at his brothers words

"Yeah you do. Great Grandma's ring. I got Grandmas, which is now on Joy's finger and you get great grandmas."

"Wait a minute, mom gave YOU grandma's ring?"

"How did I know you were going to say that? You get Great Grandma's ring, so what's the big deal? It's yours whenever you're ready."

"Which could be soon in this town," Ryan said.

Wyatt sat up straighter. There was a ring waiting for him whenever he found the one. The thing was, he was pretty sure he'd already found her. It was silly really. Here he was a single guy going about his business when one day a door opened and it was over.

Then he got to know her and he fell even harder.

Life was funny, that was for sure.

The night continued for several more hours until he got a text from Norah.

Norah:
Thank you for making me do this.
Wyatt:
You're having fun then?
Norah:
Yes but I am ready to go whenever you can get here.
Wyatt:
Give me fifteen minutes.

He nudged his brother. "Can we get out of here?"

"I take it Nora's ready?"

He pushed his chair back and stood. "Yeah, she is."

They said their goodbyes and headed for Carly and Tony's house.

He knocked on the door and waited for someone to answer. At just the thought of seeing her after several hours apart, his heart was beating faster and his palms were sweating.

The anticipation was overwhelming.

When the door finally opened, it was Joy not Norah standing in front of him.

"Look everybody, it's the Murray boys!" She threw herself at Flynn and he caught her mid air. Wyatt shook his head as they made out right there in front of him and everyone else.

"Hey, Wyatt," Carly said, one hand lying across her pregnant stomach.

He looked around the room, not seeing Norah anywhere. "Hi everyone."

"She's in the bathroom," Avery said with a smirk on her face.

"Oh okay." The ladies were sprawled everywhere, bottles of beer and wine covering the tops of tables.

"Joy let Flynn breathe, will ya!" Leah shouted.

Joy slid down Flynn's body but he didn't let her go. "I don't need to breathe," Flynn said.

"Ahhh," Carly said sarcastically. "Gag me with a fucking spoon."

"Ignore her," Julia said. "She's just mad that she's sober."

"Hey, you and I are sober too and you don't see us being all cranky," Addison yelled from where she was curled up on the couch.

"Oh yeah," Wyatt said, "I hear congratulations are in order."

Julia beamed and rubbed her still flat stomach. "Thank you."

He looked up just as Norah emerged from the hallway. Her cheeks were flushed and her hair, which had been down when he'd dropped her off, was now piled high on top of her head.

As soon as she noticed him a smile turned up her lips. "Wyatt...hi."

"Hi," Carly said, shaking her head. "That's all he gets after you spent all night talking about him. Run to him, romance movie style like you're in an airport and haven't seen him in years."

"Can someone shut her up," Mel said.

"Eat this," Dani shoved a cupcake in Carly's mouth.

"New girl's got gumption," Addison said.

"I'm not the new girl anymore," Dani said. "Norah is. Pick on her."

"Can't pick on her or Joy will beat me up."

The whole time this exchange was going on, all he could think of was that apparently, Norah had been talking about him the whole night.

That had to be good right?

Finally, she walked toward him, her purse and jacket in her arms. "Ready?"

"If you are?"

Joy hugged Norah as they were walking out the door and Flynn nodded to him over their heads.

As soon as the door closed behind them, Norah began to talk.

"Oh my God, Wyatt, I had so much fun. Thank you for telling me I could do this." She was animated, using her hands as they walked to his truck. “Those ladies are awesome all in their own way. Did you know that Mel used to dance at Julliard and that Addison is like a math genius? I found out so much stuff tonight about them all. Is that what it’s like to have friends? Who knew?”

He listened to her ramble on as he opened the truck door for her. She was still talking when he took his seat in the driver's side.

“Hey, Norah?”

“Yeah.” She turned to look at him.

“How much did you have to drink?”

Her eyes widened and she bit her bottom lip. A lip that he planned to bite himself in the near future.

“A lot.”

“Define a lot.” He started the truck and backed out.

“Can’t be totally sure but I think I finished a bottle of wine all by myself.” She reached out, placing her delicate hand on his shoulder. “Is that bad?”

He dropped his head against the headrest but kept his eyes on the road. He was ravenous for her. Wanted to do every dirty thing imaginable. But could he do those things if she was drunk?

“You know, from what Mel says, drunk sex is exhilarating. And I’ve never had drunk sex.”

He made the mistake of looking over at her and almost ran off the road by the needy desire he saw on her face.

“Do me a favor? Stop talking until we get home. Then I’ll show you exhilarating.”

He didn’t want to speed but man did he want to be home. She followed his instructions and kept quiet the rest of the drive. After he was parked though, it was game on.

“Can I speak now?”

“You’re gonna be too busy for that.” He hauled her across the console and down onto his lap. She laughed the whole way but was right with him when their mouths collided in a kiss.

They were both frantic for each other, each of them seemingly in a hurry. His hands found her ass, loving the way it fit perfectly into his hands.

"Wyatt, please," she begged and even though he wasn't sure what she was begging for, he tried his best to give her what she wanted.

His hands found their way under her sweater and without hesitation, he pushed it up and over her head. Needing to taste her skin, he pulled the cup to her bra down and latched on to one hard nipple.

"Holy fuck!" she shouted, holding his head to her chest. "Don't stop."

"We should go inside," he panted against her skin.

"No, no, no." She pulled his head back by his hair. "Know what else I've never done? Had sex in a car. You wouldn't deprive me would you?"

"I'll give you anything you want." He wanted to say that included in life, not just sex but now wasn't the time.

She smiled. "Then what are you waiting for?"

The smile more than the words kicked him into motion. Finding the button on the side of his seat, he pushed it and the seat started moving backward. It was still tight but with the seat back they had a little more room.

Norah was kissing his neck and down his chest as her hands searched his lap for the button and zipper on his pants. His own hands found the clasp on her bra, pulling it off her body.

She freed his erection, moving her hand up and down his hard length.

It was harder for him to get into her pants but somehow he managed it. Clumsily he rolled on a condom that he'd pulled from his wallet and in an instant was inside her.

"Oh yeah," she moaned.

She felt good, too good and he couldn't stop himself from fucking her hard. Well as hard as he could with his pants halfway off and her on top of him.

She did most of the work, riding him like a damn bull.

The noises she was making — moans, groans and words that he'd only ever dreamed a woman would say to him — had him on the verge of coming from the moment he'd gotten inside her body.

His fingers dug into her hips as she rode him up and down. When her back arched and she threw her head back, he pumped furiously into her, sending them both over into release.

As he came down from euphoria, it dawned on him that they were out in the open where anyone would be able to see them. Yes it was late and yes it was dark but still they were right in front of the building.

When she started to sit up, he held her to him. "Don't move yet." He scurried to find her jacket so he could cover her up.

"Put this on."

She gave him a side-eye but did use it to cover her chest. "I'm pretty sure it's a little late for modesty."

"I could look at you naked all day but we're kinda out in the open here."

She looked around, immediately shrinking on top of him. "Holy crap. I didn't even think about where we were."

"You and me both." He laughed. "Let's get out of here so we can make love in a bed with no chance of anyone seeing us."

Hurriedly, they made their way out of his truck and into the building.

Chapter 12

He'd said make love.

Wyatt wanted to make love with her.

Not sex, but love.

Not fucking but love.

Did that mean something? Was he in love with her?

God she wished. Because she was head over heels in love with him and it freaked her the fuck out.

She'd never wanted to fall in love with him. She'd tried hard not to in fact. But if she was honest with herself, she'd been in love with him almost from the start. There was no one else like Wyatt. There had never been anyone who cared for her like he did. No one who'd ever put her needs first.

And not one other person who made her feel like she was a queen.

How was she not supposed to fall in love with that?

Inside his apartment, she swayed on her feet, the alcohol finally hitting her.

"Woah, woah," Wyatt said, grabbing her and walking her to the couch. "Come sit."

"Thanks." She sat using him for help since the room was spinning.

"I'd say the alcohol has really kicked in." He stroked her hair.

"You might be right." She closed her eyes then immediately opened them when the room began to spin. "Okay, I haven't been room spinning drunk since college."

"I'm not sure if that's a good thing or bad thing."

"A bad thing. Not being this drunk means that I never had any friends who I felt totally comfortable with to let myself go."

"You do now." His fingers tickled her neck.

She wanted to close her eyes and lean into him except if she did that, the room would start spinning again. She needed to work off this drunk. And she had just the idea of how to do that.

Sliding from the couch to the floor, she moved herself between Wyatt's legs. As her fingers worked his zipper he asked, "Whatcha doin' down there?"

She looked up to him, finding his eyes black with desire. "If you don't know, then I'm afraid I can't help you." Pants undone, she freed his cock, closing her fist around him. She moved her hand up and down his length, keeping her eyes glued to his the whole time. Watching him while she gave him pleasure was almost better than the orgasms that he gave to her.

Almost.

Needing more, she lowered her head, taking the tip of him into her mouth. His intake of breath spurred her on and she licked around the head like it was an ice cream cone. When his hand gripped her hair, she looked up with her eyes silently asking him what he wanted.

"Take me in your mouth, Norah."

That she could do.

Removing her hand, she took him deeper into her mouth. Each time she lowered down, she took a little bit more until finally he hit the back of her throat. She wasn't sure if it was the alcohol or something else but she had no problem taking him all the way down her throat.

And that was no easy feat considering his size.

His hips lifted, pushing him even further into her mouth. "Suck me," he groaned.

The sound of his strangled words telling her what he wanted had her moving her mouth faster and faster. She wanted him to feel everything she felt.

"Norah, Norah," he chanted above her as he basically fucked her mouth.

She loved every second of it. And when he came, she took it all, swallowing every last drop down.

"Holy fuck," he swore as his hands loosened in her hair.

Sitting back, she looked up to him. "God I love doing that."

He hauled her up onto his lap. "You are a queen. My queen."

She raised her eyebrows. "Do I get a crown because I would look good wearing a crown?"

"I'll get you one."

She laughed, laying her head against his chest. "I'm sleepy."

"Come on sleepy head, let's get to bed." Before she knew what was happening, he'd picked her up in his arms and was carrying her to his room.

It was better than any dream she'd had of being picked up.

Because this was Wyatt.

She woke up alone with the mother of all headaches. When she turned to see what time it was, she found a glass of water, two ibuprofen and a note.

Norah,

I had a few errands to run but when I come back, I'll bring breakfast.

Wyatt

She hugged the note to her chest, closing her eyes because really it hurt too much to have them open.

He was so sweet to her all the time. It made her feel cherished, something she hadn't felt in years. Maybe ever.

She groaned as she sat up. Overindulging might be fun in the moment but it was not her friend the next day. She sipped the water he'd left her and swallowed down the ibuprofen. She had to pee something fierce so she somehow made her way to the bathroom. Realizing she was naked, she padded back to the bedroom to find something to wear. She found a t-shirt of Wyatt's on the chair and rather than dealing with her own clothes, she slipped that on over her head. Since it wasn't long enough to cover her girl parts, she rummaged around until she found her underwear from the night before.

In the kitchen, she filled her glass with more water. She had no idea how long Wyatt had been gone or when he would be back, so she wasn't sure if she should go across the hall to her own apartment or if she should stay. Making the decision to stay, she found her phone and sat down.

She had several missed text messages.

Carly:

Joy gave me your number, I hope that's okay. Could we meet up sometime in the next couple of days? I have a proposition for you.

Joy:

I gave Carly your number. No idea what she wants and honestly with Carly, it could be anything.

She couldn't fathom what kind of proposition Carly could have for her. Carly didn't know her whole story like a few of the others that she'd already told. She'd wanted to go into last night without everyone pitying her or feeling like they needed to be nice to her.

She wanted friends who liked her for her.

Norah:

When did you want to meet?

Carly:

Would this afternoon work? I can come to you?

Norah:

Sure.

She sent her address and they decided on two o'clock. Setting her phone down, she crossed her legs under her on the couch and waited for Wyatt. She didn't have to wait long though, since he came in the door a few minutes later.

"I was hoping to make it back before you woke up." He was carrying several bags of what she assumed was food.

"I've only been up a few minutes."

He set the bags on the counter before walking to her, leaning down and kissing her. "Good morning."

She pulled him in for another kiss when he would have pulled away. "I missed you when I woke up."

"Sorry about that." He smoothed her hair back from her face. "I wanted to surprise you." He stepped back. "Come eat."

"It smells great."

"I got a little bit of everything. Pick your poison."

They both pulled containers out of the bags and when she began opening them she found eggs, bacon, sausage, pancakes and hashbrowns. He slid two plates on the counter and she began filling them.

"This all looks so good. Where'd it come from?"

"There's a diner in town that only does breakfast and lunch. From what I've been told it's been around forever. The old timers meet there for breakfast at like five."

"That's so cool. Where I'm from there isn't a whole lot of tradition like that. Nor places that serve this kind of food." She snatched a piece of bacon, popping it in her mouth. "Everyone eats healthy food all the time. It gets old."

"While I'm a fan of eating healthy food, I also love a good greasy cheeseburger or in this case a fatty breakfast."

"Look on the brightside, the eggs are good for us."

He laughed, picking up both plates. "There is that." He walked into the living room, setting them down on the coffee table. She joined him with her coffee and his orange juice.

"Carly wants to meet with me today," she said as they sat down to eat.

He looked over toward her. "About what?"

"I have no idea. She texted and said that she has a proposition for me."

He took a bite of eggs, chewing and then swallowing. "I could try and find out for you if you want?"

The fact that he was willing to do that, made her all gooey inside. "No, I think I'd like to wait and find out when she comes over. But thank you. Thanks for all of this. For taking care of me when I was drunk by leaving water and medicine by the bed and for getting me breakfast and for offering to find out. Thank you for all of it."

"It's all my pleasure."

She looked at him, shaking her head. "Why is that? Why did you so easily slide into my life like you were always supposed to be there?"

He dropped his fork. "I keep wondering that too and the only thing I can come up with is that I am supposed to be here. With you. It's the only thing that makes sense."

She swallowed, wondering if she was even going to be able to speak. "I...It's insane. But all I want to do is be with you. Two weeks ago I didn't even know you and now you are all I think about, all I want. I'm starting to think I've been hiding for no reason. That maybe it's time I stop hiding and start living again."

He took her hand. "The part of me that wants you safe, never wants you to stop hiding. But in here," he tapped the side of his head, "this part of me knows that you can't hide forever."

"For what it's worth, if it wasn't for you I think I would be fine hiding forever. You make me want to live."

He dropped his forehead against hers. "And you make me want to love."

She sucked in a breath. Had he just said what she thought he said?

"I'm not saying it...yet, because I want you to be ready, to know your own mind. Just know though that those feelings are inside me. When I see my future, I see you in it with me."

Her head told her that she wasn't ready to be in love but her heart told her that she didn't get to decide. It happened when it happened.

Wyatt had some work to do, so he left her alone in her apartment. She spent the time writing, for the first time the words just flowed out of her. She'd started writing to give herself something to do and because she loved to read but now it seemed she had to write. The words had to come out. When her phone went off with the alarm she'd set, she stood and stretched her sore muscles.

She was about to grab a glass of water, when there was a knock on her door. She found Carly on the other side.

"Sorry I'm a little early, but," she rubbed her belly, "this kid is trying to kill me and I couldn't sit anymore."

She ushered her inside. "No problem. I'm guessing you don't want to sit down but how about something to drink?"

"You're a funny girl, something I noticed last night and the reason I wanted to talk to you."

"What is this proposition you have for me?"

"As you can see, I'm pregnant and in about four months there will be a baby."

"What? That's how it works. Thank you for explaining because I had no idea." She was smiling while Carly was frowning.

"Ya know, I'm starting to see why you and Joy are friends."

"I've never had a lot of friends so having Joy — and now all the rest of you — is pretty new to me."

"Can I ask," she finally sat down, "what is it that you do? Joy made us all promise not to ask questions about you and I'm cool with that but I like you and want you to do what I'm about to propose but really, I don't know anything about you."

She nodded, taking a deep breath. "I might as well tell you since several other people already know."

"Wait, people other than Joy know?"

"Yeah, Wyatt, of course and then Flynn and Dax and Avery and Leah and Brandon."

"Mother fuckers! They did this on purpose. They know how much I hate not being on the inside."

She laughed. "They didn't do it to leave you out; they kept the secret because I asked them too."

"You think that's why but really it was just an excuse for them to get back at me." She eyed her. "You're not like dying, are you?"

"I'm not dying. I am, however, in hiding from a man who possibly killed my parent's and who wants to steal the company my dad worked hard to build."

"Why am I pregnant for this because I could really use a drink."

"I can get you some water or maybe a soda. Although I'd have to go to Wyatt's for that."

"I know that you know I meant alcohol but thanks anyway. Okay start at the beginning."

For what felt like the hundredth time, she told the story. Each time it was a little easier and now she could tell it quickly, keeping out all emotion.

"Wow, I need a second to process this. And FYI, how in the hell did you ever date this Brett guy? I don't take you for an idiot."

"He was charming and did everything right. At least at first."

"How was the sex?"

"What does that have to do with anything?"

"Bad sex is a good indicator that the relationship was doomed."

Was that true? "It wasn't great."

"Like how not great?"

"He didn't like me to go down on him."

Carly pointed her finger at her. "And there it is. Believe me no guy who loves you is turning down oral sex. Even if he doesn't like it, which...that's not even a thing. All guys like it. But even if, he'd let you do it if you liked doing it."

"I like doing it." She felt herself blush.

"I was sober last night, I remember."

They had talked about everything, sex being at the top of that list and somehow in her drunken conversation she remembered mentioning how much she loved to be on the giving end of oral sex.

"So you're saying that because he wouldn't let me suck his dick I should have known he was a jackass?"

"Kinda." She said it with a straight face and Norah had no other option but to laugh. And laugh and laugh.

"Oh God if that is true then I really am an idiot who could have stopped this all from happening the first night we had sex."

"Probably not. The asshole obviously had his eyes set on you and would have done anything — including letting you suck his cock — to get you on his good side."

"Some days I feel like such a failure. Actually most of the days before I met Wyatt that's how I felt. Now I feel...empowered. Like I am strong enough to deal with this. To deal with him."

"Have you ever thought about contacting someone other than the local police out there? Maybe the FBI?"

"I thought about it but just never did it. Maybe it's time for me to do it now."

"I can help with that. Or at least Anthony can. He has a friend who is a special agent in the FBI and he will listen to you and not treat you like you are crazy."

Was it that easy? Could she talk to this FBI guy and finally have this finished?

"Stop thinking about it," Carly said. "I'll have Anthony talk to him tonight. In the meantime, let me lay out a scenario for you. When I have this baby, I'm not going to be able to work for several weeks. Twelve if Anthony has his way." She rolled her eyes. "Why do men think that having a baby means we need to stay home and do nothing for three months?"

"Maybe because it's hard on your body not to mention your emotions."

"Yeah, yeah. Maybe he has a good point. Anyway, when I take this time off, we are switching things around at the studio and Mel is taking all my advanced classes and Leah will teach all the little kids and beginner type classes. That leaves the office empty. I bet you can guess where I'm going with this?"

"You want me to work in the office?" Norah was dumbfounded. Carly, Leah and Melanie owned and operated a dance studio in town. It was one of the things she'd learned the night before.

"Bingo. We can't leave it unattended and even more I don't want Leah to have to do double the work. Teaching and all the office work."

"I'm flattered that you'd think of me but I'm not sure I'd have any idea what to do."

She waved a hand in front of her face. "You would pick it up fast and Leah would still do the real important stuff. We just need you for day to day stuff like registrations, payments and keeping the place organized."

It sounded interesting and she really liked the idea of getting out of the apartment more. But she was still afraid of Brett finding her. Of him coming after her.

"Why don't you think about it and in the meantime, I will talk to Anthony about contacting his friend. Maybe after you talk to him, you'll feel more comfortable giving me an answer."

She gave a sigh of relief. "I think that's a good idea."

"Are you okay with me telling Anthony?"

"At this point so many people know that I don't think it matters."

Carly reached out to touch her in a comforting manner. "It does matter. None of us will tell anyone who you don't want to know nor will we let you be in danger."

"I think Wyatt has that last part covered."

"Yeah, I noticed that. His Hollywood good looks will fit right in with you when you get your real life back."

She blinked, unsure why Carly would say that. Did Carly — or for that matter, everyone else — think she would up and move, taking Wyatt with her once she was safe? "I wouldn't ask Wyatt to move from here."

"So you're what? Going to have a long distance relationship?"

"I don't know. I haven't thought about it."

"You better think fast then because that man is head over heels in love with you. And if I'm not mistaken, you feel the same way about him."

She wanted to deny that he was in love with her, deny that she felt the same, but it was futile. She did love him and just that morning he'd virtually told her that he felt the same. But none of this was in the plan. She'd eventually planned to go back to California, reclaim her spot in her father's company and move on with her life.

Now none of that mattered.

Now she had Wyatt.

And she couldn't in good conscience ask him to move to California just so she could work sixty hour weeks and never see him.

Even more, she didn't want to work sixty hour weeks and never see him.

That was no relationship.

Her dad had been good at delegating, at least in the last part of his life, so he and her mom spent a lot of time together. It also helped that her mom worked at the company so they spent a lot of time together there.

Wyatt didn't want that life again. He'd had it once before and it had almost killed him.

She wouldn't ask him to do that again.

"What have I gotten myself into?"

"When Anthony and I first met, man did I hate him. He got under my skin like no other guy ever had before. But I knew, I knew without a doubt that he was going to be important in my life. That's why I fought it for so long. When I finally gave in and let myself love him," she stopped and shook her head, "it was the best thing in the world. Didn't matter that my life was in upheaval or that it had only been a week. All that mattered was that he loved me enough to be by my side no matter what." She stood. "Now you have to decide. Is choosing your old life worth losing this new one?" She walked to the door. "I'll be in touch."

Norah watched her walk out the door and thought about her words. When she'd picked up and ran from her old life, she figured she'd had nothing to lose. But now, if she left Cedarville it was the opposite.

She had the most important thing in the world to lose.

Chapter 13

By the time Wyatt arrived back home, he was exhausted. Anytime he had to deal with the bank he felt drained. But he was trying to secure a loan so he could purchase another building in town. The other two, the apartment building and the building that housed Joy's salon, had been funded with his own money. Well his and Flynn's.

But there was another building on the market and he'd like to have it to help with income. And the nice thing about the new building is that it was in perfect condition. There would be no need to do updates which meant all money would immediately go to paying back the loan.

Win win in his analytical mind.

When he walked in the door, the first thing he noticed was that it smelled amazing. The second was that Norah was in his kitchen, dancing to the loud music as she cooked.

Closing the door quietly, he leaned against the wall and watched. She was open and free and oh so beautiful. Some days he still didn't understand how it came to be that she was in his life. He was nobody special but she was amazing.

The most amazing person he'd ever met.

He felt so undeserving of her attention.

Not wanting to be creepy and continue to watch her, he cleared his throat loudly. She immediately turned her head.

"Hey, welcome home."

Home. His and hers.

God that sounded good.

"Smells delicious."

"Thanks." She turned back to her task. "It's just an easy chicken parmesan but I thought it might be nice to cook for someone other than myself for once."

"I'm impressed. Much to my mom's dismay, I can't cook. And when I say can't, that's what I mean. I've tried and failed many times. My mind doesn't seem to understand that recipes don't have to be exact."

"My mom used to cook all the time and taught me. She always said a woman should know three meals off the top of her head not including breakfast food."

"Sounds like a smart woman."

"She was." She opened the oven, sliding in a pan. "Now we wait."

"Are you going to leave me in suspense? What did Carly want?"

"Oh that. Actually she wants me to help out at the dance studio while she's on maternity leave."

"Teaching?"

"God no. Leah would switch into teaching and she wants me to work in the office."

"Does she know about your past?" They hadn't had much time to talk the night before and he'd been wondering if she'd told everyone.

"She does. I just told her today because I thought she should know if I decide to take her up on her offer. Both for her sake and because I wanted her to know why'd I'd possibly say no." She took a sip of the wine that she had sitting on the counter. "What do you think?"

"I think you should do whatever you want."

"Come on, Wyatt. I need your opinion. Should I do this?"

He sighed and poured himself a glass of the wine she had opened. "I'd worry that the more people who see you the more you might get recognized. That in turn would make me worry for your safety. But I also know realistically that you can't hide out forever. At some point you are going to have to attack this head on."

Her face was unreadable and he had no idea what she was thinking. Until she closed the distance between them, gripped his head in her hand, pulled it down and kissed him.

"That's the exact right answer."

When she tried to pull back, he grabbed her around her waist, holding her to him. "If it's the right answer, then where do you think you're going." He kissed her again, this time longer and hotter.

"I have more to tell you," she said when they came up for air.

He reluctantly let her go. They each grabbed their glass of wine and headed for the couch.

"It seems Tony has a friend who works for the FBI. And after Carly and I talked, she mentioned him and asked if I'd ever thought about talking to someone other than the local police."

"Did you?" He wasn't sure what he thought of that.

"I never had before but I think I'd like to. If Tony and Carly trust him, then maybe it's time I try to get my life back."

Her words stunned him. She wanted her old life back. The one in California. The one that didn't include him.

Fuck.

Of course she wanted that life back. Who wouldn't. He'd been deluding himself thinking she could enjoy life in the small town of Cedarville or that she'd ever love him.

She was going to leave.

And he'd be alone again.

Always alone.

"I think that's great." He knew his voice sounded flat and emotionless but he just couldn't make himself fake it any better.

"Wyatt," she touched his leg, "you do know that it's just a conversation right? Nothing is going to happen overnight and even if it does, that doesn't mean anything."

"I want you to have your old life back. To be able to come and go as you please, dye your hair back the color it was, do any job you want, but I don't," he stopped shaking his head, "I don't want to lose you."

"You're not going to lose me." She scooted even closer to him. "I don't know what's going to happen but I know that I want you in my life. We can figure it out right?" Tears started to fall from her eyes. "Please tell me we can figure it out."

He took her into his arms. "Of course we can." He wasn't sure if the words were truthful even though he wanted them to be. He would never stand in her way to get her old life back. She'd lost too much in life and deserved to have everything she wanted.

He just wasn't sure if that included him.

The next day he made the drive to Woodridge to meet with Tony. Before Norah made contact with Tony's FBI buddy, Wyatt wanted to make sure it was the right thing to do. He found him in his office, sitting at his desk.

"Wyatt, hey," he stood to shake his hand, "I'm pretty sure I can guess why you're here."

"Yeah, I wanted to talk to you before anything else happened."

"Have a seat." They both sat. "I was shocked speechless when Carly told me Norah's story. That poor girl has been through the wringer."

"Tell me about it and she's still so amazingly optimistic and happy. It blows me away."

"Carly is not easily impressed and Norah impressed her."

"So this friend of yours, is he reliable?"

"Derek is the best. We met in college and have stayed friends ever since. From day one in college, he always wanted to be in the FBI and he worked hard to get there. He didn't come from money or a police background, so it took a lot of grueling work to make it. But he did and since has worked his way up to special agent."

"And you trust him?"

"Absolutely. I texted him last night and asked if we could talk about something, off the record. He agreed and said he'd call me today."

"I'm just worried about her. Worried that this jackass will find her and hurt her."

"I get it, believe me, I do, but Derek won't let that happen. He's a good guy and more, he's my friend. He will do everything in his power to help."

"I'm counting on that to be true." Wyatt stood.

"Before you go, I took the liberty of talking to Brandon last night so I could gather what information he had compiled on Norah. After looking at it and then doing some searching, my instinct tells me that this Brett guy did in fact have something to do with her parents' deaths. Or if not him, someone."

He sat back down. "What does that mean?"

"Once we talk to Derek, if he agrees, my guess is they will investigate. From there who knows. This guy is obviously smart and if I had to guess he didn't physically do anything himself but hired someone. But if Derek can prove it, he'd go to jail."

He exhaled, finding relief for the first time in hours. "That would give Norah her life back."

"That's the hope."

Yeah that was the hope.

He left Tony's office, driving back to Cedarville. Instead of going home though, he went into town, parking in front of Joy's salon. Only he didn't get out. He dropped his head forward onto his steering wheel.

He was happy things were moving forward for Norah. Happy she was on the way to getting her life back. But what did that mean for him? He'd heard her when she'd said nothing would change for them, but he was having a hard time believing it. He'd do almost anything for her but moving to California to live a fast paced life again...he didn't think he could do it.

It had almost killed him last time he'd lived that life.

If she asked though, he'd do it for her.

He loved her that much.

Love.

He'd told her he was close when in reality he'd been in love with her after the first time they'd met. She had that much power over his heart.

It belonged to her.

He looked up when he saw out of the corner of his eye, someone walking toward him. It was Joy.

He rolled down the window.

"What the hell are you doing sitting out here?"

"Trying to figure out my life."

"Well come do that inside." She walked away.

He could either get out of his truck and follow her inside or he could leave and go home where he'd have to talk to Norah.

Shaking his head, he pulled the keys from the ignition and opened the door.

Inside the salon, he found Joy sitting in one of the chairs she used for pedicures. "Come sit. Soak your feet in the water."

He raised his eyebrows. "I am not getting a pedicure."

"First, don't be so negative about pedicures just because you're a man. Men get pedicures. Second, I'm not giving you a pedicure but you are going to soak your feet. It's relaxing. And from the looks of it, you need to relax."

He looked at the water then back up to her. "What do I do?"

"Take your shoes and socks off, roll up your pants and sit down."

He did as she said, sitting and then slipping his feet into the warm soapy water. "Okay, so this isn't so bad."

"It's gets better." She pushed a few buttons on a remote looking thing that was attached to his chair and all of a sudden the chair began vibrating.

"Oh wow." It felt amazing. "No wonder women get this done all the time."

"We are no dummies." She leaned back against her chair and he did the same. "Whenever you are ready, you can tell me what's wrong?"

He stayed silent for what felt like minutes. He let himself relax, let his body decompress. Finally he spoke.

"Norah is going to talk to Tony's FBI friend."

"And I'm guessing this freaks you out?" Her voice remained calm.

"What happens," he raised his voice but then settled it, "what happens if she gets her old life back and then leaves?"

She turned her head against the chair to look at him. "Would you have given up getting to know her, falling in love with her all because it might end? And don't even try to deny being in love with her."

"I am in love with her, that's why I'm so afraid of her leaving."

"But would you give that up? Is your world not a better place just having met her?"

"Of course it's better but that doesn't mean that I want her to leave."

"Duh. But I'm not asking that. There are no guarantees in this world, Wyatt. But every day I thank my lucky stars for the days I've gotten to spend with Flynn. If he perishes tomorrow, I know that my life has been better because of him."

He closed his eyes. "Of course my life is better and I'd never want to go back to the days where I didn't know her but how can I live without her?"

"You don't know that you'll have to. I've seen her with you, listened to her wax poetic about how awesome you are. She's in just as deep, Wyatt. How do you know that she'd leave?"

"She left her whole life behind and hid herself away from the world for almost two years. Not to mention that she owns one of the world's top software companies. Who would choose me over that?"

"You're selling yourself pretty short. You have a lot to offer her, most importantly love. And take it from someone who never knew how big love could be, it's a fucking huge game changer."

"So what am I supposed to do in the meantime?"

"You make sure she can't live without you that way when she has a choice to make, there won't really be a choice."

He dropped his head back down against the chair. Make himself indispensable to her. He could do that. But how.

As if she could read his mind she said, "Just keep doing what you are doing. Be there for her. Be supportive. Be caring. But most of all be loving. She'll be putty in your hands."

"Is that what you did with Flynn?"

"Ha! More like that's what he did with me. After several days of being with him, I couldn't imagine my life without him. It really pissed me off."

He rolled his eyes. "I can imagine."

"You don't even know. Flynn is insistent. Add in that he's funny, smart, hot as hell and has a beard that turns me on, I was a goner."

"Please," he put up his hand, "I do not want to hear how my brother turns you on."

"Whatever. I had to hear all about your sex from Norah last night so the least you can do is listen to me."

"You guys really talk about that stuff. In detail?"

"Yup." She grinned widely. "Let's just say I know way more about you than I ever thought I would."

He grimaced. Having his soon to be sister-in-law know the things he'd done with Norah somehow wasn't at the top of his list of things he wanted her to know.

She was drying off her feet which she had been soaking along with him. "Give me a few minutes and I will get you a towel and freshen up your feet."

"Wait. What?" What was she planning to do to his feet?

"Just relax. I'm not going to paint your nails or anything. I'm just gonna buff your feet and moisturize. Trust me, you'll love it."

He wasn't sure about that, but once she started, other than the fact that at first it tickled, it really did feel amazing. As she worked, he thought about everything she'd said. And she was right, as usual. If Norah was no longer in his life, he'd be thankful for all the time he'd gotten to spend with her. She made him into a better person.

"All done," she announced.

He looked down at his feet and somehow, they not only felt different but they looked different. "Thanks. I think."

"Give it a day or so and you'll realize how good it feels. You'll be back."

He began to put his shoes back on. "Do you do this to Flynn?"

She pursed her lips. "Maybe."

"He told you not to tell anyone, didn't he?"

"Maybe."

"I'd say I'd give him hell but now that I know how good it feels, I can't in good conscience make fun of him."

"Believe me, he's secure enough in his manhood to take all the ridiculing you can dish out."

"And I'm not?"

She shrugged. "I guess we'll find out."

Laughing, he walked to the door. "Thanks for talking it out with me."

"Anytime."

Outside, he paused looking up at the sky. Instead of dwelling on the what ifs, he was going to set it aside and live each day he had with Norah, while at the same time making himself so crucial to her life that she would have no choice not to leave him.

He was going to make her realize that leaving him was the worst decision she could ever make.

Chapter 14

It had been hours since she'd seen Wyatt and she was pretty sure she was having withdrawals.

It felt like she needed him to breathe and wasn't that just freaking fabulous. She'd gone and fallen in love with Wyatt Murray. She didn't want to need him, didn't want to feel him in her soul but that's the way it was. And she was pretty sure she was going to want to stay in Cedarville when all was said and done.

Other than her mom and dad, she'd never felt as if she fit in out there. She'd always felt that she was a misfit in a world full of popular people. While not everyone was fake or unfriendly, a lot were. And that just wasn't her. She liked being nice. She liked talking to people randomly.

She was born to live in a small town.

Born to live in Cedarville.

On Dragonfly Lake.

Dragonflies.

Something her mom and her had loved together.

It was like her mom had brought her to this wonderful world knowing it was where she was supposed to be.

The question was, did Wyatt want her to stay?

Dropping her head back, she slid down on the couch to get more comfortable. She'd been basically pouting all day about not seeing Wyatt and it wasn't getting any better.

There was no way she could move back to a place she barely liked where she'd have to live without him everyday.

She'd rather live with him in a place she hated than to live in a place she hated without him.

And yes, she knew she was making a life decision based on a guy which was something she swore she'd never do in her life but really it wasn't about him. It was about her and how she was finished living a life that didn't suit her. She wanted to enjoy life. To wake up everyday and make a difference. And then go to sleep every night next to the person who helped make her happy.

Wyatt and Cedarville.

They went hand-in-hand.

Even if he didn't want her like she wanted him, she still wanted Cedarville. And that meant she wasn't making a decision *only* based on a guy.

She was deciding what she wanted for her future.

When she heard what she knew to be the front door to the complex opening, she jumped up, going to her door to check the peephole. Before she could even put her eye to the door though, there was a knock.

She still checked, paranoia still alive in her body, and sure enough it was him. She couldn't open the door fast enough.

"Hi," he said, looking better than he had a right to look.

Her mouth went dry and all she could think about was him and how much she'd missed him. And how much she loved him.

She definitely couldn't say that last one.

Reaching out, she pulled him inside, closing the door and pushing him up against it.

"Missed me, did ya?"

Wrapping her hand around his head, she pulled it down toward her and latched her mouth to his. He tasted...he tasted like home.

She heard herself moan into his mouth, or maybe it was him that moaned. She couldn't be totally sure but it didn't really matter.

"Norah," he murmured her name as he turned them so that she was against the door. "God the things you make me feel."

"Tell me," she panted out. "How do I make you feel?"

He stopped moving, his eyes searching hers. "Out of control but at the same time calm because you are in my arms. I want to be with you all the time, it's practically all I think about and that's insane because

I am an adult not a fifteen year old teenage boy who can't control his hormones."

She smiled and ran her hand down his face. "I wish I'd known you as a fifteen year old boy. I'd love to have been on the receiving end of your hormones."

He leaned in, running his tongue along her bottom lip. "We would have been that couple that everyone hated. Making out everywhere we went."

She ran her hands over his shoulders. "I would have liked that."

He lifted her up, helping her wrap her legs around his waist. "Being adults is much more fun. We could have never done this at fifteen."

He spun them around, walking through the living room, her holding on for dear life. "Thank God for adulthood."

By the time they made it to her bed, both of them were somehow naked. With ease he slid a condom on and within seconds was inside her. For the first time since they'd been together, they moved slowly, taking their time loving each other.

It was different. It felt different.

Like they were in the same place. Wanted the same things.

She prayed that they wanted the same things.

After, with both of them breathing heavily, she laid her head on his chest, making circles on his skin with her fingers.

"Don't disappear on me again."

She felt his hand come up to stroke her hair. "I won't. I just had to...think."

"I figured. And I get it. I needed to think too." She lifted her head to look at him. "I want to meet with the FBI agent. I want to find out what he thinks and what can be done. I badly want to start living again. But I don't want to do any of that without you. I need you to be there, next to me, with me while I figure it out."

"I'm not going anywhere. I'm here as long as you want me."

It was on the tip of her tongue to tell him that she'd always want him but she kept it to herself.

"As much as I'd like to stay here in bed with you all day, I have to go upstairs and check on a problem that someone is having."

She flopped back down on the bed. "Fine. Go. Just leave me here all by myself."

He rolled on top of her. "Don't pout. I'll come back and when I do, maybe I'll bring you a treat." He kissed her lips gently, lingering.

"What kind of treat?" she murmured against his lips, latching on to his head with her hands.

"You'll just have to wait and find out." He gave her one last kiss then rolled off her, standing up next to the bed.

She watched him as he dressed, admiring how his muscles rippled as he pulled his pants on. He wasn't built like a bodybuilder, more like a swimmer. Long and lean.

"If you keep looking at me like that, Mrs. Masterson is going to be waiting a long time for me to look at her leaky sink."

She met his eyes, biting her bottom lip. "Maybe I have a leaky sink."

He stood, bare chested, hands on his hips looking down on her. "I won't be gone long."

Grabbing the pillow from behind her head, she threw it at him. "You suck."

He threw it right back at her. "When I get back, I promise I will make it up to you." He finished dressing, kissed her goodbye and left.

And once again she was alone.

Only this time, she knew it wasn't permanent. Wyatt would be back.

Forcing herself from bed, she showered, dressed and cleaned up her room. Including new sheets for her bed. In the kitchen she cleaned up a little before deciding that she was bored.

In all the time she'd spent alone the last two years, she'd never really felt bored. She'd known what she was doing was to stay safe so she'd been okay with it. But now that she had Wyatt, being alone was not as fun.

Grabbing her phone, she texted Joy.

Norah:

I'm bored.

Joy:

I assumed you'd be canoodling with Wyatt?

Norah:

We already did that and now he's working but I'm bored.

Joy:

I just finished my last client. Give me a few and I'll stop by.

Norah:

You don't have to change your day for me.

Joy:

I'm not doing anything else. Be there soon!

She set her phone down laughing. How she'd gone her whole life without a friend like Joy, she had no idea. It was important, she was realizing, that having friends you could count on was more important than having love. Those were the people who helped get you through when love went sideways.

She really hoped she didn't need Joy to help her get through anything like that.

Her parent's deaths didn't break her. Brett abusing her didn't break her. But if she lost Wyatt, she wasn't sure what she'd do. What kind of person she'd be.

Joy showed up thirty minutes later but she wasn't alone. Julia was with her.

"I brought reinforcements," Joy said as they both walked inside.

"While you're always welcome," Norah said to Julia, "I don't think my boredom is a dire situation."

"My day was over anyway and I happened to be at Joy's salon when you texted."

Julia and Joy sat on her couch and she sat on the old chair that she'd picked up at a yard sale beside them.

"Where's Wyatt?" Julia asked.

"He had to help a resident with a leaky sink." She sat back in her chair. "God I'm such a mess. A month ago, I was fine all alone every day. But now I can't go an hour or two by myself."

"Cut yourself some slack," Julia said. "You've gone through some big changes and to go from having a life where you had friends and family to then living like a hermit, well it's only natural that when you get some semblance of normal you will latch onto it with a tight grip."

"While I'm not trained in this like her," she pointed to Julia, "I understand what she's saying. If I had to guess it's like a person who has to go without water for days on end. Once they get it, even though they know they are supposed to sip slowly, they just can't."

"Yeah I guess that makes sense, I just hate that I feel so needy."

"That's love," Julia said. "No other way to describe it. When Wes came back into my life, I was drawn to him like a magnet. When we were apart, all I wanted was to be back with him. It will go away after a while. Mostly."

Joy scoffed. "Mostly my ass. You two are always together."

"I'd make a comment about you and Flynn except I don't think it would be healthy for the baby if you punched me."

"I would never punch a pregnant woman."

Julia raised her eyebrows, looking over to Norah. "I'm not sure I believe that."

"Me either."

"Hey!" Joy yelled, crossing her arms over her chest. "You should be nicer to me."

"I'm nice," Norah said. "Very nice. Everyone always told me so."

"That's probably part of your problem." She raised her eyebrows. "Maybe you need to stop being nice and start being real."

"Did you just quote The Real World?" Julia asked. "How do you even know that? You are way too young."

"I used to hide away when I was like twelve and watch it. I loved that show."

"While I can't say I watched it," Norah said, "even I know the phrase."

"The phrase has merit. Being nice is good and all but sometimes that can get you into trouble. Like in your case. If you had been a little less nice, the situation with Brett might have never happened."

"But then I would have never met Wyatt." The words were out of her mouth before she could even think.

"Good point," Julia said. "And, way to look on the bright side. You have to find the good inside the bad sometimes and it looks like you are realizing that."

"I hate that I let a man control me. That I gave him that much power and didn't walk away right when it started. But damn if I'm not going to learn something from it. Wyatt is the best thing to happen to me. Ever. And I'm not going to let him get away."

"You might want to tell him that," Joy said.

"I did. I think." Hadn't she?

"Are you sure about that? I don't want to break confidence here, but the man is a mess. He thinks that once you settle this situation you will go back to California and leave him."

She was speechless. He was worried about something that was never going to happen. "California will always have its place for me, but this place, Cedarville and more importantly wherever Wyatt lives, is my home now."

"This is like the best love story ever written," Julia said. "Well except for mine and Wes's. But second best is still pretty good."

"You might want to think about being more transparent when it comes to talking to Wyatt. He's already been through a lot and while I didn't see him when he first moved here, the way Flynn describes him is not pretty. He was on the verge of killing himself from overworking. He doesn't need to add any stress to his life."

She stood up, needing to move. "I don't want to add stress. I want to take it away. Make him relaxed and happy."

"Talk to him," Julia said. "Make sure he knows that you are on the same page."

"I will." She turned to stare at her friends. "I most definitely will."

"Okay, can we talk about me for a minute," Joy asked.

"Yes, yes, yes," she said and sat back down. "Anything to not think about my life."

"I am stressing out about this wedding. Avery is amazing and helping a ton but I'm starting to wonder if I have cold feet. I just don't want to do any of the prep."

"Want my professional opinion?" Julia asked. At Joy's nod she kept going. "You don't have cold feet, you just don't want to do any of the work. You're not a person who cares if everything is perfect or pristine. You just want Flynn."

"And you," she turned toward her, "what do you think?"

"I don't know you as well, but I tend to lean the same way as Julia. You aren't nervous about marrying Flynn."

She bit her bottom lip. "I just hate that I'm not more excited about the actual wedding. But when I think about my life, I always picture Flynn, so yeah, maybe I don't have cold feet."

"Not planning your own wedding is pretty normal. At least where I come from." She shrugged. "I've known women who never even picked out their own dress. You should do what you are comfortable with and not worry about anything else."

"Wise words," Julia said. "I doubt Flynn cares whether it's you or Avery who plans the wedding. As long as it's you standing at the end of the aisle, he'll be happy."

"Oh it'll be me and as for the dress, I picked that sucker out and I look fucking amazing in it. His jaw will drop to the floor."

"You got a dress and didn't tell me?" Julia asked.

She grinned. "Oops."

Julia threw a pillow at her. "Oops my ass."

"If it makes you feel better, I haven't shown anyone. Not even Avery. Something about everyone seeing me for the first time on the day of my wedding appealed to me."

"That, my friend, is planning your wedding."

A smile lit up her face. "Really?"

"Yes, really," Julia said. "You made a decision on something that will happen on your wedding day."

"I feel so...accomplished."

They all busted out laughing. It was nice to have friends and even nicer to know they had your back when you needed them.

Chapter 15

Fixing the sink in Mrs. Masterson's apartment had taken longer than he'd anticipated. Probably because he wasn't a plumber. But he'd learned enough from his brother and YouTube the last few months to make him decent.

Decent did not mean fast.

After he finished, he showered and changed before knocking on Norah's door.

She opened it in a hurry.

"Didn't you get my messages?"

He felt for his phone which wasn't there. "I must have left it in my place."

"Carly texted. Tony's friend Derek is in town and wants to meet with me."

"Tonight?" That was fast. He wasn't sure he was ready.

"Apparently." She moved back inside her apartment. "They asked if we could come by around seven. Does that work for you?"

"You want me to go with you?"

She stopped what she was doing, turning to look at him. "Of course I do."

He swallowed the lump in his throat and nodded. "I wasn't sure."

She moved fast, coming to stand right in front of him, cupping his face in her hands. "Wyatt, I want you with me. Always. And when this is over. I'm not going anywhere."

He searched her eyes. "Do you mean that?" He gripped her wrists. "Because I want you and want to be with you but I'm not sure if I can move again. I can't live that fast paced life again."

"You won't have to. I love it here. Have felt more at home here than I ever did in California." She lifted onto her toes and kissed him lightly on the lips. "You aren't getting rid of me."

He rubbed his lips together, relishing her taste on them and knew that this was as good a time as any.

"I love you."

She smiled. "I think I figured that out but it's still good to hear."

He inclined his head. "That's all I get?"

"Oh did you maybe want me to say it back?" She was playing with him, he could tell.

"You don't have to say anything that you don't want to."

"That's good but this, this I want to say. I love you, Wyatt. So, so much."

He kissed her as soon as the words left her mouth, taking everything she gave him. She tasted of mint like maybe she'd just brushed her teeth but underneath was all Norah. Sweet, charming, strong, independant Norah.

"We don't have time for this," she said against his mouth. "We have to get to Carly and Tony's."

"Later."

"Most definitely."

He stepped back, afraid that if he didn't, they'd never get out of there. She loved him. Him.

She. Loved. Him.

Life was good.

"Let me go grab my phone, keys and wallet and we can head out."

"I'll be ready."

And she was. They drove the few short miles to Carly and Tony's where he pulled in and turned off the truck.

"You ready for this?"

"I am. It's just talking right? If he doesn't think anything can be done, then it'll be over. I'll just live out the rest of my life in hiding, here with you."

"Why do you not sound so excited about that?"

"I want it to be over. I want to walk out into the world without ever worrying that Brett is out there to get me. Someday I want to get married, under my real name and have kids who I can talk to about my parents and all that they built." She turned her head to look at him. "I didn't say any of that to freak you out but I'm done not saying my truth."

He grabbed her hand. "Nothing you say freaks me out." He lifted it to his mouth, kissing her knuckles. "Let's go in and see what he has to say. That's the first step. We can deal with everything else as it comes."

They walked onto the porch, Tony letting them inside the house after they knocked.

"Thanks for doing this on such short notice, guys. Derek showed up here without warning and seemed really interested in talking to you as soon as possible."

"Anything to see what we can make happen," Wyatt said, his hand on Norah's lower back.

"Come sit. Derek had to take a quick call but will be right back out." They moved into the house, he and Norah taking a seat on the couch. "Can I get you anything to drink?"

"Water for me," Norah said.

"I'm good right now," he told Tony.

"Is Carly still at work?" Norah asked.

"Yeah, she should be here in about half an hour though."

Before Tony could return with Norah's water, a man came down the stairs. "You must be Norah and Wyatt," he said, coming around the couch.

"Nice to meet you," Norah said and shook his hand, Wyatt following suit.

"Sorry, my boss is riding my ass and I had to take his call." He cringed. "Sorry for the language."

Norah laughed. "You're fine."

"Not to jump right in, but I'd love to hear your story from your mouth."

Norah looked at him. "Sure."

Wyatt listened to her tell the whole story from start to finish. Derek took notes but didn't butt in. He held her hand, squeezing for comfort when she'd take breaks. He hated for her to keep going over and over it, but knew that it was needed if she wanted to regain her life.

"Okay, wow," Derek said. "That's even crazier hearing it from you." He looked at Tony. "I thought Tony and Carly were just exaggerating. I mean, Tony not so much but Carly, I could see her stretching the truth."

"This story needs no exaggeration," Norah said. "It's my life."

"Let me tell you where I'm at. First, I believe everything you are saying about Brett Dalton. Even if I hadn't done any checking into him, what I've seen on TV would have been enough for me to distrust him. He's not a genuine man. Everything he says is to manipulate people. I've been trained on what to look out for and he has all the markers."

Norah let out a breath. "It feels so good to hear someone say they believe me."

"Then you're gonna love what I have to say next. I talked to a friend of mine in the California office and you just might be in luck. They have been investigating Dalton for over a year."

"What?" She looked over to him, her eyes wide.

"It seems that when you tried reporting him, the police couldn't do anything because their hands were tied, not because they didn't want to. They were told to drop the case by the FBI since they already had a case going against him."

"It wasn't because they didn't believe me?" She had a hand to her chest and was breathing heavily. Wyatt could see the relief on her face and it made him want to hold her in his arms.

"Nope. They believed you but had to act as if it was no big deal."

Since she didn't say anything, he took the lead. "So what's happening now?"

"They have plans to arrest him for not only the planned murder of your parents where he hired someone to run them off the road but also the planned murder of two other people. It's a pretty big case and from what I can tell, the evidence against him is rock solid. He's going to go to prison for a long time."

"So I'm free?"

"I wouldn't say that, at least not yet. Nothing moves fast in law enforcement. It could be months or even a few years before it's all said and done. But for all intents and purposes, you are in the clear."

She turned to face him. "Did you hear that? It's almost over."

"I heard," he swept a piece of hair off her relieved face.

"There's a few more things. The FBI has been looking for you."

"For me?"

"They want to talk to you and from what it seems they want you to testify."

She stiffened next to him. "I can't testify. Oh God and now they know where I am."

"Hold up. They don't know where you are. I'm talking to you as a friend of Tony's not as an FBI agent. Nobody knows I'm here. All the inquiring I've done has just been as an interested party. If you choose to stay hidden, that's up to you. But Norah, if you come forward with what he did to you, it's going to make the case stronger. So strong that he'll likely never get out of prison."

"I don't know that I can."

"What if I told you that you aren't the only woman he hurt."

"There are others?"

"There are always others. A man who abuses never only does it to one person."

Again she looked at him, her eyes asking him what she should do.

"You have to decide this yourself. This isn't and can't be my decision. But if you want my opinion, I'll give you that."

She nodded.

"You can do this and you should do it. Not because he scares you or because you're afraid of him, but because you aren't. Because he didn't break you. Didn't ruin you. You are stronger than him. Bigger than he will ever be. Show him how strong you are by making him small and unimportant in your world."

She kept her eyes on his as she said, "I'll do it. I'll come forward and testify."

"I think you're making the right choice," Derek said and nodded to him for his help in convincing Norah. "I will make some calls and see what needs to happen." He stood but before walking away stopped. "For what it's worth, Wyatt is right. This guy is the type that will hate that he didn't break you. He gets off on doing just that."

He walked away, leaving just them and Tony in the room.

"You were right," Wyatt said to Tony, "Derek is a good guy."

"He's not the type who would pressure you or go behind your back. That's just not the kind of person he is."

"Thank you so much for putting us in touch with him."

"Anytime, although now that I say that I hope you never have the need for the FBI ever again."

"You and me both," Norah said, laughing.

Carly chose that moment to burst through the door. "I'm here!"

"Yes, honey, we hear that." Tony walked over to her, removed her bag from her arms and kissed her. Wyatt heard a whispered, "missed you" and reveled at the love they shared.

"Holy cow my feet hurt. Why doesn't anyone ever tell you how bad your feet will hurt when you are pregnant?"

"I'm gonna wager that not all pregnant women dance on their feet for six hours a day," Norah told her.

"You make a good point." She slipped off her shoes and sat down in one of the two chairs next to the couch. "Okay, what'd I miss?"

"So fucking much," Norah said on a long breath attached to a laugh.

"Beer?" Tony asked him over their heads.

He gave Norah's hand one last squeeze and then stood. "Hell yeah."

While the girls talked, he and Tony moved to the kitchen where Tony handed him a bottle of beer. He took his fist sip just as Derek walked in.

"Where's mine?"

"Coming up," Tony said.

"How long have you known Norah?"

"Only a short while. Couple of weeks or so."

"Wow. You guys moved fast."

"I saw her and I knew."

He shook his head. "You and Tony both. This fucking town."

"My suggestion, only move here if you're ready to settle down."

"That might be a problem."

"What?" Tony handed him a beer. "Are you moving here?"

"My boss wants me to stay here and watch out for Norah once we announce that she's not in fact, dead."

"That's great news!" Tony slapped his back. "It'll be great to hang out more."

"I doubt that an almost new dad will have a lot of time to hang out."

"I'll make time. But you should heed Wyatt's warning. Single people don't stay single here for long."

"I'm in love with my job. There's no time for more than that."

"You say that now but just wait," Wyatt said.

"Tony," Carly called from the living room, "I'm hungry."

"Who's up for some pizza?"

"Count me in," Derek said.

"Me too," Wyatt added. He looked out to Norah to see if she was cool with staying. She nodded, completely understanding what he was asking.

As Tony walked away to order the pizza, he and Derek talked.

"This guy, Brett Dalton, he's a master manipulator. You are going to need to keep a close eye on Norah once we reveal she is alive and well."

"You won't give away her location though, right?"

"No. Never. But that doesn't mean he won't find her. He's a madman who will do anything to get what he wants."

"I won't let her out of my sight."

"Tony mentioned that Norah lives in a building you own. Any chance there are any vacancies? It would help to be as close to her as possible."

"There is nothing available right now but I think we might be able to work something out. My place is right across the hall from Norah's. If she is okay with me staying with her, you can stay there."

"It could be months."

Months, living with Norah.

Yes please.

"I'll check with her, but I don't see it being an issue."

"Here's my card, just let me know either way."

Wyatt pocketed the card as he walked into the living room. Carly was telling some funny story about a kid she taught in class and laughter lit up Norah's face.

"Speaking of kids," Derek said, "Where's Reed?"

"He's with Addison and Ryan tonight," Carly answered.

"I still can't believe that Addie is married, raising a kid, with another one on the way. I remember her as a fourteen year old, albeit gorgeous, teenager."

"Yeah, yeah Addison is gorgeous. We all get it."

"You're beautiful to me, babe." Tony kissed her head.

"You have to say that because I'm carrying this big headed baby of yours around all day long."

"How do you know it's big headed?"

"All babies are big headed when a woman has to push them out of her vagina."

"Here here!" Norah raised her water in agreement.

Wyatt sat down next to her, once again taking her hand in his. Happiness was radiating from her, making her face even more beautiful than she already was.

He loved seeing her like this. Happy. He just loved her period. And when this was all over, he couldn't wait to see who she became.

Chapter 16

Breathing heavy, Norah rolled off Wyatt and onto her back.

"Way to make good on that promise from earlier." As soon as they'd walked in the door to her apartment, he'd had her in his arms. Within minutes they'd been naked, in bed and making love.

"Seems like you reciprocated nicely." He was also breathing heavy, his chest rising and falling to the beat of his heart.

"God, I feel so...invigorated!" She stood up and spun around the room. Even though everything with Brett wasn't one hundred percent settled, she still felt free. Or at least more free.

She looked over to Wyatt, who had rolled onto his side, his hand holding up his head. "Enjoying the show?"

"Hell yes, I am."

She hopped onto the bed on her knees, her boobs practically in his face. "It's almost over. I'm going to get my life back, Wyatt."

He brushed his hand on the underside of her breast. "You can do anything you want."

She moaned. "This will be at the top of the list."

He laughed, his fingers trailing over her nipple. "Have you thought about what you'd want to do?"

"Other than this?" She sighed at the feel of his fingers on her skin. "No idea. I've never let myself go there. Never wanted to get my hopes up."

He stopped what he was doing. "Now you can start thinking about the future."

She pushed him so he was flat on the bed, throwing her leg over his body until she was straddling him. "Right now my future is all about this." Leaning down, she kissed him, her tongue tracing his lips. Her hands roamed his chest, loving how he flexed under them. Just as she was about to go lower though, his phone rang.

"What the fuck." He reached out to grab it. "Who is calling this time of night?" It wasn't that late but it was after eleven.

She slid off him and listened as he answered. "Hello."

His face creased as he listened. "I'm on my way." He dropped his phone. "Mrs. Masterson's leaky faucet turns out to be more than that. I've got to go check it out."

She frowned. "Mrs. Masterson is a real cock blocker."

He laughed. "That she is." He got dressed then bent over to kiss her. "Get some sleep. I'll be back soon."

He walked away and she dropped back down on the bed. They'd had a good night. A great night really. Knowing that soon Brett could be behind bars and she could live again gave her renewed strength.

She was getting her life back. The company that her dad had built from scratch would be there for her. She didn't want to run it, never had, but it would be hers again to do with what she wanted. The money would be there to help as many people as she could. Which is what she'd always wanted to do anyway.

Be useful. Do good. Make the world a better place.

And now she'd be able to. With Wyatt by her side.

Two days later, she was helping Wyatt move some of his things into her apartment.

They were going to live together.

At least while Derek was there to watch over her.

It felt odd but in a butterflies in her stomach kind of way. They were together all the time and spent all their nights sleeping in the same bed. Those were the reasons he'd given her when he'd suggested it.

What she'd wanted to hear was that he loved her and wanted to live with her. Not that it was needed to protect her.

That just kinda pissed her off.

Didn't mean that living with him wasn't still an exciting moment for her.

"Where do you want me to put my clothes?" He asked, standing in the doorway to her bedroom.

Well, their bedroom now.

"I made some space in the closet and drawers. There was actually plenty since I don't have that many clothes."

He dropped the items he was holding onto the bed. "We can change that now."

She shrugged. "I don't want to spend all the money I have left just yet. I'd rather wait until I know this is over."

"What if we spend my money?"

"I can't let you do that, Wyatt."

He reached out and pulled her toward him. "Maybe I want to spend my money on you."

"You don't have to do that. I have everything I need." She ran her fingers through his hair. "You're all I need."

"You say that now but what happens when you get sick of me?"

"Not going to happen."

"I'm gonna hold you to that." He kissed her lips, taking the kiss deeper second by second.

"While I love where this is going," she said as he kissed down her neck, "Derek is on his way over with an update."

His lips stopped on her collarbone. "Someone or something is always in our way."

"It does seem that way, doesn't it?" She shoved him away. "Put your clothes away and I'll go make sure there is room on the couch for us to sit."

In the living room, she moved a few things off the couch so there would be room to sit. As she was folding a blanket, a knock sounded on the door. Like always she checked the peep hole just to make sure it was Derek before opening it.

"Hey, come on in."

He walked past her into the apartment. "Looks like you guys are still settling in. I hope this was really okay with you?"

"It's all good," she said with a happy face. "We are together all the time anyway."

Wyatt came out of the bedroom. "You get your stuff moved in?"

"I travel fairly lightly. Some clothes and my laptop is all I need."

"Must be hard, always being on the road."

"You get used to it." He took a seat on the couch. "Mostly."

"Do you ever get to see your family?" she asked as she sat down.

"I don't have much family. My dad raised me but he passed away about three years ago. No siblings or grandparents. No aunts or uncles. It was just dad and me and now it's just me."

"I'm sorry." It sounded stupid saying it outloud but what else did you say to that information.

"Nothing to be sorry for. Dad lived a long, happy life where he got to see me live out my dream."

"Tony mentioned that you'd always wanted to be an FBI agent," Wyatt said.

"Since I was about seven."

"All I wanted to do at seven was follow my brother around and steal his Hot Wheels."

Derek laughed. "Hot Wheels were pretty high at the top of my list too."

Her hands fidgeted in her lap. "I guess we should get down to it, huh?"

Derek took in a breath. "The press release went out this morning about you being alive. The agent in charge of the case is keeping an eye on Dalton to make sure he doesn't leave town or talk to any known criminals."

"And they didn't say where she was, correct?"

"No. They only said that she was found alive and in FBI protection. Now comes the hard part. We need you to make a statement...about why you left."

"You want me to tell my story? About Brett?"

"Yes, and I know that's going to be hard but we think it will get the public on your side. Right now it looks like you just up and left. A disgruntled girlfriend."

"What?" She stood up, looking down at Wyatt. "People think that?"

"I'm sure that can't be true," Wyatt said.

"We don't know for sure but the people at the company think that. And most of them loved Brett and were confused when you up and left after making it so he couldn't have any say. It's part of his manipulation. Part of how he gets people to love him."

"So now it's my job to convince people that he's a monster?" She paced around her apartment.

"It's not your job. We just think it will help. The info we already have on him is going to make people think twice about him. But you know how the media is, how they can easily distort things. Any and every piece of evidence against him is going to get the public on our side."

She stopped moving, understanding what he was telling her. Her story was going to help the world understand what a bad person Brett was.

"All right. I'll do it." She sat back down next to Wyatt. "Under protest."

Derek smiled. "The sooner the better."

She rolled her eyes. "I will do it tonight."

"Is there anything else?" Wyatt asked.

"Not really. I'm here for you though, Norah. If you leave the house, I need to know about it. I will follow, at a distance, always staying out of your way. We don't won't anyone to know I am here."

"Anyone meaning Brett."

"Him or anyone he might hire, which is more likely. He doesn't like to get his hands dirty."

"No shit." She was starting to get pissed.

Finally.

It had taken a lot of days, a lot of hours of thinking she had been the problem. Only now was she realizing that it had nothing to do with her.

"Can I say something as myself and not as an FBI agent?"

"Sure." She cringed having no idea what he could want to say.

"Women like you, the ones that get out, any way they can. You are my heros. I will never understand men who hurt women and it took me a long time to understand why women stay. Why they feel they can't leave? But the ones who do," he shook his head, "you're just amazing."

She softened. "It's hard being that woman when you know inside that you are stronger than that. But it's scary to leave, to give up everything you know, for a freedom that's not really freedom."

"This will all be over soon, I promise. And in the meantime, I will help keep you safe." He stood. "As I am sure Wyatt will. Remember to keep me in the loop whenever you leave the apartment." He walked out of the apartment, leaving it just her and Wyatt.

"What are you thinking?" Wyatt's hand was stroking her back.

"That this is all so insane." She turned to face him. "I still wonder how I was stupid enough to take up with a guy like Brett. I had reservations about him from almost the start. But he was so...slick and came across like he truly cared, so I put aside my first instinct. There's a lesson there. I should always listen to my instincts."

"I think everyone should. We have them for a reason. But what I was asking is what are you thinking about writing the statement?"

"I'm thinking that it sucks that I have to open myself up to scrutiny just to make it known what a bad man he is. But I'm also thinking that if my statement helps one woman to not fall into the trap of a man like him, then it's a small price to pay."

"Have I told you lately how much I love you?"

"About thirty minutes ago." She winked, laughing.

"What if I go make us some dinner while you work on your statement?"

She frowned, sagging her shoulders. "I guess I should but is it really safe to eat anything you make?"

"I'm thinking grilled cheese. That's pretty idiot proof."

He got up and she grabbed her laptop from the table in front of her. Needing silence, she popped in her earbuds and hit play on a playlist of songs that relaxed her. It was a mix of songs her parents had loved, some she loved and some she'd heard in TV and movies. When the first song came on she was immediately transported to a time when she was seven or eight and her mom had taken her to the zoo. She closed her eyes, remembering the sounds and smells of everything that had been around them.

Her mom had been so beautiful even in her old clothes which was what she had been wearing that day. It hadn't been a planned trip, but one that happened on a whim after her mom had gotten frustrated with painting her bedroom.

She'd thrown down the brush, put her hands on her hips and declared that it was too nice a day to be inside painting. Wearing the same clothes she'd painted in, they'd driven to the zoo. For hours they'd laughed and played, not caring who was watching or that they were supposed to be doing other things.

When they'd gotten home, her dad took one look at them and fell into a fit of laughter that his wife, who he'd never known to leave the house not perfectly made up, had gone to the zoo of all places, in her painting clothes. Her mom had declared from that day forward that she'd care less about how she looked and care more about how she felt.

And she'd kept that promise.

When Norah looked down at her computer, she realized that she'd written half her story already while she'd been thinking of her mom.

Maybe it wouldn't be so hard after all.

Song after song came and went as she poured her heart out through her fingers. She told of how he'd been nice at first, sweet even. How he treated her well. Then how everything had changed in the blink of an eye.

She couldn't be friends with guys. Could barely even have female friends. How he sucked up to her dad when he was around but behind his back, badmouthed him to her, trying to get her on his side.

She just kept going and going until finally, she got to the day she'd walked out the door, afraid for her life, afraid she'd never be herself again, but happy to just be alive.

Not wanting to look at it again, she shut her laptop and pulled out her earbuds.

It was done.

She looked over to the kitchen, where she found Wyatt watching her as grilled cheese sizzled in the pan.

"Watching you while all those emotions played across your face, that was hard for me."

"It was hard for me." She set her laptop aside and stood up. "But it's finished."

"That was really fast." He flipped a sandwich.

"The words just poured out of me once I got started. It was almost...cathartic."

"Good. I was worried it would set you back. Telling the story to people is different than writing it all down."

She leaned against the counter, her head resting on her hands. "Would you like to read it?"

He looked up. "Only if you want me to?"

"I think I do. I don't want to read it again but someone needs to so I know it's okay to give Derek." She stood, reaching out to take the spatula from his hand. "I'll do this, you go read. The password is dragonfly. Capital D."

He paused. "Was it always dragonfly?"

She nodded. "I'm pretty sure my mom knew I'd need this place one day. Need you."

She watched the grilled cheese sandwiches while he read. It was like waiting for ice to melt, wondering what he was thinking. Had she revealed too much? Was it written horribly? While this was not one of the books she'd been writing, she still wanted people to feel the emotion of her story.

Finally, he looked up.

"So?"

"God, Norah." He set the laptop aside. "I've heard your story half a dozen times and I'm still speechless at what I just read. You are a phenomenal writer. This is what you should be doing. I know this story is not something you are proud of, but you should be. And reading it is so much more powerful than hearing it. You weave words and emotions together like it's music."

His compliments on her writing embarrassed her. How did you say thank you when someone was giving you such an amazing compliment?

"Any woman who reads this, hell any person who reads it, will never doubt what kind of person he was."

She breathed a sigh of relief. Hearing that what she wrote could be helpful made it all worthwhile.

Somehow, Wyatt was in front of her, holding her. "You are a miracle. My miracle."

For what felt like the first time since her whole world went up in flames, she let go. She sobbed in his arms, with him holding on and taking it all. Taking all her pain and all her sadness.

When the tears dried up, all that was left was relief and happiness.

Chapter 17

A week passed in blur and all of a sudden Thanksgiving was upon them.

It had been eight days since the FBI had released Norah's statement. Eight days and nothing.

No weird people in town. No calls or emails. No news on the investigation of Brett Dalton.

Nothing.

Just the two of them living together, enjoying each day they had together.

And he loved it.

But he knew it couldn't last.

The other shoe was bound to drop.

They were on their way to Logan and Melanie's house where a huge group of people would be celebrating Thanksgiving together. It was going to be loud and crowded, something he didn't overly love but that Norah was looking forward to. She'd never had a big Thanksgiving with lots of people.

He was going to give her whatever she wanted.

"It's hard to believe it's Thanksgiving with how warm it is outside."

"Welcome to weather in Ohio." It was over sixty degrees out and had been for the last two days. "Nice weather means we get to play football."

"Melanie said we'd be playing football even if it was cold."

"Good thing it's warm then." He pulled up to the house parking behind several other cars and trucks. Looking behind him, he saw Derek pull into the driveway.

"Let me come around and help." She was holding a pie that she'd made along with a bottle of wine.

He took the pie from her lap, then shut the door behind her after she got out. "You know, I didn't celebrate Thanksgiving last year, or the year before."

"What did you do?"

"Nothing. I ate what I normally ate, did what I normally did. It was just another day."

"That's gonna change today. Today you can do all the things you want to do."

She stopped walking at the bottom of the steps. "All I want is to spend the day with you and my new friends."

"That's an easy one." He leaned over to give her a kiss.

Inside they found a large group of people already there mingling around.

"Oh, you made pie," Carly said, taking the dish from his hands. "I love pie."

"You love everything," Melanie said from behind her.

"Hey, can I help it if this baby is hungry all the time."

"You know, when this baby is born, who are you going to blame for things?"

She shrugged. "I'm sure I'll find someone. I mean babies can't talk. I can blame it."

Norah laughed. "That will be some great parenting."

Melanie looked at Wyatt. "Shoo."

"Excuse me?"

"What she means is go away," Carly said. "We can't talk about you if you are standing right here."

He rolled his eyes. "I'll go see what the guys are doing." He gave Norah a kiss. "Enjoy," he said sarcastically.

He walked away and found Tony and Logan on the deck, each drinking a beer. He looked around but didn't see his brother.

"Flynn's not here yet?"

"I haven't seen him," Brandon said. "Was he supposed to be here?"

"No, but I'm pretty sure I saw Joy in there."

"Oh yeah, she came early with Avery. Something about a Thanksgiving pedicure. Apparently it's a tradition." Logan shrugged.

That was new to him, but he'd be sure to ask her about it. He grabbed a beer from the cooler against the wall.

"How's having Derek around all the time?" Brandon asked.

"It's not the worst. He keeps to himself mostly. Today will be the first real interaction we've had with him since he first moved here."

"Makes sense that he doesn't want people to see him with you or hanging around."

"It's a little odd to know we are being followed all the time." He took a sip of his beer.

"I hear you guys are living together," Logan said. "Is that gonna be a permanent move when this is all over?"

"Hell if I know. Would I like it to be? Fuck yeah, but I have no idea what Norah is thinking."

"Why not ask?" Logan said. "Be direct in your feelings."

"I thought I was being direct, but she was weird when we talked about it. Sometimes I wonder how men and women ever stay in relationships with how confusing they can be."

"They aren't confusing if you communicate. She can't read your mind just like you can't read hers. When you tell a story you don't start in the middle and assume she knows the beginning do ya? No, you tell the whole thing. That's what you need to do when you talk to her. Pretend she has no idea where you are going with what you are asking. Treat her like a complete newbie. Takes out a lot of guessing."

Brandon was staring at Logan. "What the hell, bro. When did you get so smart?"

"I've always been smart, jackass. That's what happens when you sit back and watch and listen to everything going on around you."

"Is Logan out here giving relationship advice again?" Flynn walked out onto the deck. "He's like the love guru."

"I will take that title and run with it." Logan flipped him off.

Wyatt reached in the cooler to get a beer for Flynn and handed it to him. "So Logan has given you relationship advice?"

"I'm pretty sure everyone in this damn town has given me relationship advice."

"At least you guys had help. When I met Leah the only person I had to talk to was my mom," Brandon added. "And while I love my mom, talking to her about love and sex and anything to do with that, is not high on my list of things I want to do."

"Poor baby," Logan said, slapping him on the back.

All heads turned when they heard a new voice step out onto the deck. "Is one more allowed out here," Derek asked.

"Come on out," Wyatt said.

"Yes, come out and tell us all about Tony when he was younger?" Brandon said. "I'd love to have something to hold over him...and maybe something to torture Carly with."

Derek laughed. "Tony was pretty much always the way he is now. Friendly, helpful, nice." He paused. "God he's so nice. It's kinda annoying."

"Carly sure as hell didn't think he was nice when they first met," Logan said.

"I disagree," Brandon said. "She thought he was nice which was why she hated him."

"Pretty sure Joy felt the same way about me when we met," Flynn said.

"Which explains a lot," Wyatt said, "because from what I can tell, they are exactly alike."

Everyone laughed...at least until they heard a throat clear behind them. Turning they found Joy and Carly, both with their arms crossed.

"See," Carly said, "I told you they'd be gossiping."

"Looks like I owe you twenty dollars."

"It's scary how alike they are," Brandon said. "One was enough but two," he fake shivered, "that's too much."

"Are you gonna stand there and not defend my honor?" Joy said to Flynn.

"Come on, babe, you know damn well the way you are. You like it even."

She pursed her lips. "He's got me there."

Flynn pulled her toward him, circling his arms around her back, gripping her ass. "Plus, I like you just the way you are."

"Ugh," he groaned. "Get a room."

"Don't mind if I do," Flynn backed her into the house.

"Do not have sex in my bed!" Logan yelled after them.

"As for the rest of you," Carly said, "there are appetizers in the living room."

Brandon and Logan walked into the house and Derek said, "She scares me."

"Join the club."

"Thanks for inviting me to this. A home cooked meal sounds fantastic right about now."

"Don't get many of those, I'm guessing."

"Not really. I can cook the basics but nothing that would be considered home cooked."

"Thanksgiving is my favorite holiday. While I love all the food, what I really love is the pie."

"I saw a bunch of those on the counter."

"Yeah, which is why I'm out here." He pointed to the cooler. "Can I get you a beer?"

"I wish but until this is settled, I'm on duty twenty-four-seven."

Wyatt appreciated that he took his job seriously. "That's gotta suck though. It's not always like that, is it?"

"Thankfully, no. Most of the time, I work normal days where I get time off."

"I appreciate you doing this then. It can't be easy."

"So far it's been peaceful. I kinda wish I was here in the summer when the lake is open. Not that I'd be able to take advantage."

"You'll have to come back."

"Maybe I will."

"We should go grab some of that food before it's all gone." They walked inside the house to find it even more crowded. From the looks of it everyone was there.

He greeted several people as he grabbed a piece of cheese off a tray. He saw Wes and Julia across the room and went to say hello. As a bonus, Norah was talking to Julia.

"Hey guys," he said as he walked up to them.

Wes shook his hand. "Wyatt, good to see you."

"You actually get a day off."

"He gets four," Julia said. "He closed Dockside for the whole weekend."

"Wow, what will the town do?" he mocked.

"They will deal." He pulled Julia in close to his side. "My wife and I needed some time off."

"Good for you guys," Norah said.

"Any more news on the investigation?" Julia asked Norah.

She looked at him. "Not that we've heard. As far as we know, Brett is still in California."

"And we're hoping it stays that way."

When Wes and Julia walked away, Norah pulled him down the hallway. "Is something wrong?" he asked as she found an empty room and pulled him inside.

"Something is very wrong." Her eyes held mischief and when she pulled his head down to kiss him, he finally got what she was saying.

"Oh, I see now." He backed her up until her legs hit the bed.

"Watching you out there, from a distance, seriously turned me on." She sat down, immediately working on the button and zipper of his pants.

A strangled laugh bubbled out of him. "I wasn't doing anything particularly sexy."

She looked up at him but her hands kept working. "You are always sexy." She freed his cock, stroking him from base to tip. "Have you ever done this?"

He swallowed, her hand on his cock making it hard to speak. "Define this?"

"Had your dick sucked at a party."

He shivered from her words and somehow managed to answer. "No"

She inclined her head. "A first for both of us then."

Her tongue came out and licked the fluid on the head of his cock, forcing a moan from him. "Norah." He wasn't sure if he was asking her to stop or begging her to keep going. All he knew was that it felt amazing.

And when she took him fully inside her mouth, his knees buckled at the feeling. He watched as his cock disappeared into her mouth again and again. She'd change it up, sometimes, licking the head for several seconds and sometimes keeping a bobbing rhythm. She used both hands, one at his base and one teasing his balls.

But it was when she licked the underside of his dick, her tongue touching his balls that he lost control.

Gripping her head, gently, so he wasn't forcing her, he pumped in and out of her mouth. She dropped both her hands and let him fuck her mouth, each time, the head hitting the back of her throat.

After a few pumps, he came, his release pouring down her throat.

"Fuck me," he said on a whisper.

She stood, patted him on the shoulder and walked past him. "My work here is done."

Quickly, before she opened the door, he pulled his pants up. "What about me, I mean you." He was still hard at just the memory of what she'd just done to him and was salivating at the thought of doing the same to her.

She stopped at the door, her hand on the knob. "Later." But before she could open the door, a knock sounded.

"Melanie would appreciate if you wouldn't have sex in her house," they both heard Carly's voice through the door.

Norah pulled it open.

Carly stood there, arms crossed with a smug look on her face. "Just as I suspected."

"We did not have sex," Norah told her.

"Really? Then explain this." She reached out and touched Norah messed up hair where his hands had been.

Norah batted her hand away. "Don't you have anything better to do."

"Not really." She looked over Norah towards him. "Anthony is looking for you."

Walking toward them, he brushed his knuckles down Norah's cheek. "Later," he whispered, kissing her.

He found Tony in Logan's office. "What's up?"

"I have a proposition for you?"

"I feel like I should be afraid."

"It's not that serious. I'm thinking about buying a building here in Cedarville. A place to house a second office so both Addison and I could be closer to home once the babies come."

"What do you need me for?"

"I know this is your kind of thing and at first I was thinking of one small space but I found this," he flipped a photo around on the desk for him to see, "and thought maybe you'd want to go in on it with me."

He picked up the photo. "Where is this?" It was a building that housed several storefronts, most of them empty.

"On Maple. Carly said that when she was growing up she remembers there being a drugstore there along with a video rental place and a tanning bed salon type place. And possibly other things."

"Who owns it now?"

"According to Brandon, the town owns it. Back in the day, the owner of the drug store owned the whole building but then they put the new pharmacy on Main Street and he closed this place down. From there, all the other places closed. It's not really a street trafficked kind of place. But for an office, it would be great. And maybe other businesses would think that too."

"Like a town revitalization." He looked up to Tony.

"That's what I was thinking."

"How much is it?"

"I don't have that info yet. It's not even technically on the market, but I can't imagine that the town wouldn't want to do something with it, especially if it brings in revenue."

"I'm not sure if I can swing this right now, but I'm definitely interested. This could be huge for the town."

"That's what I was thinking. There is no rush. I doubt I'll hear anything soon. Give it some thought."

"Thanks for thinking of me. This would be a huge investment." He handed him back the photo.

Walking out of the room, he couldn't help but continue to think about the building. The apartment building was one thing and Joy's salon was just one space inside a strip mall. But a whole building that would house several offices or stores could be a huge money maker.

Only at the moment, most of his money was already tied up.

He wanted this though. Having another source of steady income would ensure his future.

A future he was greatly looking forward to.

Chapter 18

Being caught by Carly immediately after giving a blow job was not one of her finer moments.

And it only got worse when Carly decided to spill the beans.

"I said no sex in my house," Melanie practically shouted.

"Technically," Avery used air quotes, "they didn't have sex."

"If she gets off on a technicality, then so do I," Joy said. "Because what Flynn and I did in your bathroom was not full penetration."

"Oh my God!" Mel screamed. "What is it with those Murray brothers and keeping it in their pants?"

"Flynn kept it in his pants," Joy pointed out. "It was my pants that were off."

"To be fair," Addison said, "I've had sex in this house."

Mel's face froze, her mouth wide open.

"Me too," Julia raised her hand.

"What is happening and when did my house turn into a brothel?"

"Probably about the time you moved in," Leah said. "Brandon and I had a real good time in your basement."

"Same," Carly high-fived Leah. "Although not Brandon because, well because he's my cousin. But Anthony, he knows his way around a basement."

"You can stop being a prude now," Dani said to Mel, "because I know for a fact that you and Logan have had sex in both his gallery and your dance studio."

"Oh, I've done both of those too!" Carly shouted.

"Is this like a perverse game of never have I ever?" Addison asked. "Because I can't drink and that's a shame."

Hoots and hollers went up all around as they all began to laugh.

"I have a lot of catching up to do if you've all had sex everywhere in this town."

"Seems like you're figuring it out," Julia said. "Just stay out of my house."

"Have you thought about my offer?" Carly asked when everyone else had walked away. "About working at the studio?"

"I have and I think I'd like to try it." She still wasn't sure but with Derek in town watching over her, it didn't make any sense to not do it.

"Awesome. Maybe next week you can come in a few hours here and there so Leah can start getting you up to speed."

"I'll talk to her and set something up."

When dinner was over and everyone was stuffed beyond belief, she and Wyatt headed for home. She didn't realize how exhausted she was until Wyatt woke her up after she'd fallen asleep on the ride home.

"Stay there and I'll come get you," she heard him say in her sleepy state.

And then there he was, opening the door and picking her up in his strong arms. She snuggled into his warm body, wrapping her arms around his neck. She must have dozed off again because the next time she woke up, she was in her bed.

And it was seven in the morning.

She'd fallen asleep on him.

Literally.

Rolling she found him still asleep on his back with his arm thrown over his head. He was so handsome. His face held several days worth of growth which she didn't mind. Although she prefered him clean shaven. His chest was sprinkled with hair here and there, and his arms were lean muscle.

Smiling, she snuck out of bed, careful not to wake him.

She loved that he'd taken care of her. That he hadn't cared that she'd fallen asleep on him. Now she wanted to do something for him.

She found all the ingredients for pancakes and got started making them. When they were finished she stuck them in the oven to stay warm, then sat on the couch and turned on the TV. When her face popped up, she about choked.

There on the screen was Brett, giving an interview about her.

She listened to him emotionally talk about how he was so happy she was found alive but the things that she was saying about him were absolutely not true.

He'd never hurt a woman in his life and definitely not her. He'd loved her. Mourned for her when he'd thought she'd been dead. And now that she was alive, he wanted nothing but the best for her. But she was unstable, obvious by the fact that she ran away.

She stared at the screen long after his interview was over. The fucking nerve of that guy. How dare he insinuate that she was unstable.

He'd abused her both mentally and physically. And yet she was the bad guy. For leaving when she knew it was leave or die.

She was done.

Standing, she stomped across the room, pulled open the door and then pounded on Derek's door.

"Norah." He was out of breath when the door flew open. "What's wrong?"

"That fucking jackass was just on the news saying that I was crazy. That I'm unstable."

"Oh." His body seemed to relax. "I thought it was something serious."

"This is serious. I am not crazy or unstable. He's an abuser and I will not let him get away with this."

"Where's Wyatt?" He looked around her.

"He's sleeping."

"Come inside. We don't need to be screaming in the hallway."

She followed him in, still angry. "What can we do about this?"

"We're doing everything we can, Norah. Dalton is just trying to get the public on his side, same as we were with the letter."

"But it didn't work. No one even seems to care that he's the reason I left out of fear for my life."

He gripped her shoulders. "People do care. They do. I promise. We knew this could take time, that nothing was going to happen overnight. If I had to guess, Dalton is getting nervous."

She swallowed. "What if I went on TV?" It was a crazy idea and she knew it would be exposing herself.

He dropped his arms, inclining his head. "I —" He stopped. "That's not a bad idea. But why would you want to do that?"

"Because I want him to suffer. I want him to understand what it felt like for me to give up everything." She shook her head. "I want him to hurt."

"Let me talk to my boss. See what he thinks. In the meantime, try to relax. Everything is going as planned."

He opened the door where they both found Wyatt, fist up like he was ready to knock.

"Oh thank God," he said and pulled her into his arms. "When I woke up and you weren't there, I thought the worst."

"I saw him on the news. Brett."

He pulled back. "What did he say?"

She huffed out a breath. "It might be easier to find it online and watch it."

"I'm guessing I have it in an email." He walked away, both she and Wyatt following.

He opened up his email and sure enough he had the link. As they watched, she paced behind them, not wanting to see his face again.

"That asshole!" Wyatt shouted when it was over.

"Yeah he's definitely trying to gain public approval." Derek hit end on the video.

Wyatt turned to face her. "Norah you know this is him freaking out right? Nothing he said is true."

"I know that. But he doesn't get to call me crazy. He doesn't get to write my narrative." She turned to Derek. "I want to go on TV. I want him to see my face."

"What are you talking about?" Wyatt asked.

"Norah mentioned before you got here that she wanted a chance to tell her side."

"But you told your side, in your letter."

"It's not enough," she told him. "He needs to see that I am strong, that he didn't break me."

"Of course he didn't break you and I will stand behind whatever decision you make. I just want you safe."

"And I want my life back."

She blew out a breath and stomped out of Derek's apartment, over to her own. She knew this wasn't Wyatt's fault and that she shouldn't take it out on him, but it was hard when he hadn't lived through what she had.

She heard the door shut and looked up to find him standing by the couch.

"I wish I had a magic wand that could make this all go away. Or at least the words to tell you that I understand where your anger is coming from."

"I'm not mad at you, I just can't seem to control my anger for him right now. He made me seem small and weak when he spoke about me and I am neither of those things."

"Don't you think I know that? You are the strongest person I know and not just because of this situation. But because it's who you are. If I had met you on the street three years ago, I would have been able to see how strong you were. It's a part of you."

She dropped her hands from her face. "If it's part of me, how did I let this happen? How was I so blind?"

"You weren't blind and you didn't let anything happen. He's at fault here. He's the broken one."

She looked down at the floor making circles on the carpet with her foot. "I wish my mom was here. She would know what to do."

He was right in front of her now. "I know I'm a poor substitute for her, but I'm here for anything you need."

She smiled, shrugging. "I made pancakes before," she waved an arm in front of her body, "before all that."

He kissed her nose. "Pancakes sound delicious."

Needing something to do, she went to the oven and took them out. The syrup, butter and everything else they'd need were already on the table.

"Sit and enjoy." She went back and grabbed him a cup of coffee, black how he liked it.

"When I got up and couldn't find you, I was out of my mind."

"As soon as I saw the segment on the news, I rushed across the hall without even thinking."

"I wish you would have come and gotten me first." It wasn't hurt in his eyes, more concern for her life. Another reason why she loved him.

She reached across the small table and took his hand. "Next time, I promise."

He squeezed her hand. "Are you still shopping with the girls today?"

"That's the plan. Carly is picking me up at," she turned her head to look at the clock, "oh shit, she'll be here in thirty minutes."

"Go," he told her. "I'll clean this up after I finish eating."

"You're the best." She jumped up from her chair, kissing him quickly. "Love you!"

As fast as she could, she showered and dressed. She didn't wash her hair because there just wasn't time. She heard a knock on the door right when she finished pulling her boots on. Grabbing her jacket, purse and phone, she joined Wyatt and Carly in the living room.

"I'm ready," she announced. "Let me just tell Derek that I'm leaving." She sent him a text letting him know it was time. She'd given him a tentative time the night before and he'd said he'd be ready.

Her phone dinged with the reply that he was ready.

"I'll text and let you know when I'll be home." She gave Wyatt a quick kiss goodbye.

"Have fun and be safe."

"Yes, dad," Carly answered as she opened the door for them to leave.

In the hallway, they found Derek, ready and waiting.

Norah was used to him following her so she said hello and then tried to ignore him.

"I can't believe we are shopping on Black Friday," she said to Carly as they got into the car. "I've never done this."

"Seriously?" Carly started the car. "That right there is crazy. Shopping on Black Friday is a right of passage."

"Yeah in California, shopping is a hassle all around. The drive alone is torture."

"You're in for a treat then." They pulled up to Leah's house where they picked up both Leah and Melanie.

"Let's get this show on the road," Leah practically sang when she got inside the car.

They drove to Woodridge where they met up with Dani and Joy. Avery, Julia and Addison had decided not to join in on the fun shopping trip.

They laughed and giggled as they shopped, sometimes buying something, sometimes just browsing. She found Wyatt a cool picture to hang on his wall that she hoped he'd love and also a new flannel. He was always wearing the same one and while she loved it, seeing him wear one she'd bought him might be nice.

"You should try this on," Leah told her. She was holding up a cute sweater that would be form fitting and very low cut on her.

"It is cute." She fingered the material.

"As an added bonus," Carly said, "Wyatt will get to look at your cleavage whenever you wear it."

"There is that." She took it from Leah and held it up in front of her. "I should go try it on."

"Yes," Dani said. "And show us so we can oh and ah."

Laughing, she went in search of a dressing room. Finding one, she went inside and took the stall in the back. She was thinking about Wyatt and what they could do that night when a hand clamped down over her mouth.

"Don't even think about screaming," a voice she knew well, one that haunted her dreams, said in her ear. "Thought you could hide from me in this crap town, did you. Well guess what, you aren't as smart as you think you are."

Terror coursed through her veins. Where was Derek? Why hadn't he seen Brett.

Then she thought of Wyatt and their life together and the fear that had been there was replaced by anger. She wasn't going to lose the life she loved. Not this time.

Knowing it was now or never, she pushed back hard, making Brett slam into the door to the changing room. That threw him off just enough that she was able to bite his hand, forcing it off her mouth. Mouth free, she screamed as loud as she could, hoping everyone in the place heard her.

"You little bitch," Brett said and reached for her again. Just as his hand came out to slap her in the face, the door to the changing room was kicked in and there was Derek, gun raised.

"Stop right there!"

Brett stopped, his head turning.

Everything after that happened so fast that Norah could barely take it all in. One second Brett was there, the next he was gone. Immediately she was surrounded by her friends, who carted her out of the store.

She wasn't functioning all on cylinders but she knew what she wanted.

Wyatt.

She wanted Wyatt.

Chapter 19

Norah had only been gone two hours when his phone rang.

He thought nothing of it and because he was busy, let it ring without answering or even looking at it.

But when it started ringing again just moments after it had stopped, he knew something was wrong.

Reaching for it, he saw it was Derek and panic rose in his throat.

"Derek, what is it?" he answered.

"Norah is fine," were his first words. "But you need to get here now. Old Town Plaza, in front of the department store."

Before he could even hang up, someone was knocking on his door. He found Brandon on the other side.

"I heard. Let's go, I'll drive."

He rushed out the door not even grabbing a coat or caring that he didn't have his wallet or keys. None of it mattered.

Only Norah.

"What happened?" They were already in Brandon's cruiser speeding toward Woodridge.

"I don't know all the details yet, but Norah was in the dressing room and Dalton cornered her."

"Where the hell was Derek?"

Brandon shrugged. "Like I said, I don't have all the details.'

The twenty minute drive into Woodridge felt like a hundred years. He pictured every worst case scenario and the only thing keeping him sane was that he knew Norah was safe. When they pulled up, he practically jumped out of the car before Brandon even stopped. He didn't see Norah right away but did see her friends. As soon as Joy saw him racing toward their group, she moved to the side and Norah emerged.

When he reached her, he took her in his arms wanting...no needing to feel for himself that she was safe.

"I'm okay," she whispered over and over in his ear.

"What the hell happened?" he asked when he was finally able to release her. He looked up and saw an all torn up expression on Derek's face.

"I was in the dressing room and I must not have locked the door because the next thing I knew Brett was in there with me."

"How the hell did this happen?" he shouted to Derek.

He took a step toward them. "He must have already been inside the women's dressing room before Norah went back. I didn't go back with her thinking that..." he paused. "No excuses. I should have been there."

"Wyatt," Norah touched his chest. "He came when it counted, that's what matters."

He sighed, running his fingers over her cheek. "Tell me the rest."

"He covered my mouth with his hand and told me not to make a sound. I reacted almost immediately and pushed back against him so that he hit the door hard. When his grip over my mouth loosened, I bit down on his hand and then screamed as loud as I could. That's when Derek came."

"I'm just sorry I wasn't there earlier. This never should have happened."

"We don't know that he would have shown himself if you had been there, Derek. Now you have him in custody."

"How are you so calm?"

She turned back to face him. "Because he didn't hurt me and now it's over." She smiled up at him. "Wyatt, it's over. Think about what that means?"

He took her hands in his. "No more hiding."

"No more hiding." Her eyes sparkled. "I can do anything I want. Go anywhere."

For a second he worried again that she'd leave but before his thoughts could get out of control, Norah stopped him.

"After I get everything settled with the company, I want to move here permanently. Well not here but Cedarville. And I thought maybe I could help you with your business...in between writing books."

He had so many questions but the first one was, "You want to be a writer?"

She nodded. "Somebody recently told me that I had a way with words."

"And you want to do that here? With me?"

"Wyatt, I want everything with you. Anything you can think of, I am game."

He reached out, picking her up and spinning her around. "I want it all too." He kissed her as they spun, never wanting to let her go.

And he wasn't planning on it anytime soon.

Also by Bree Kraemer

The Only Series

Cedarville Novels

An Unexpected Home
Capturing Us
Choosing You
Better Together
A Chance Worth Taking
Forever Starts Here (Novella)
After All These Years
Won't Let You Down
Say When
Something To Lose
Finally Home

Friends & Brothers

Sky High Love
Bridge To Love
When It's Love

Rockstar Romance

The Right Note (Big City Heat Anthology)
Pick Me

Christmas Novella

Light Me Up

The Beckmeyer Family

Hooked
Sparked
Shocked
Kneaded

Be sure to sign up for my newsletter at www.BreeKraemer.com[1] to stay up to date on all new books, sales and freebies! And follow me on FaceBook for more fun stuff. www.facebook.com/breekraemerauthor[2]

1. http://www.breekraemer.com

2. http://www.facebook.com/breekraemerauthor

Read on for the first chapter of An Unexpected Home, book 1 in the Cedarville Series.

I'm almost home, Leah, told herself as she passed the welcome sign for Cedarville.

Home.

A word that held a complete new meaning to her today than it had a year ago.

Home, she realized, was not just a place you slept or kept your things. It was more than that. It was a place where you felt comfortable and wanted. Even loved.

It was sad that at twenty-seven years old, she was just figuring out that sometimes home wasn't where your family was.

And that is why she was on her way to Cedarville, Ohio at three in the morning.

She took a quick look at her phone to make sure she was still headed in the right direction. Not that she needed to though. Cedarville was a small town and even though she had only been there twice, years ago, she had no doubt that she could find her way around.

Cedarville was surrounded by the huge Dragonfly Lake on one side and acres of woods on the other. The only way to get in or out of town was to take Main Street right through the middle. The first time Leah had visited the town had been during the summer after her freshman year of college. Her roommate, Carly, had grown up in Cedarville and invited her to visit. Leah had a few moments of culture shock when she had first driven into town. She was from New York City and while she'd been to places like the Hamptons many times, Cedarville was not the Hamptons. It was like nothing she had ever seen before except maybe on television.

Everyone knew everyone else or at least it seemed that way. And people were nice. Like really nice. Almost nauseatingly so.

So nice apparently, that when her life had turned to shit, her friend and college roommate told her to get her ass to Cedarville ASAP. She swore to Leah that this was the place to hide out and reinvent herself.

And while Leah knew that hiding from her problems was not going to solve them, the idea that she could maybe reinvent herself is what had her packing up her car and heading out of New York.

Besides, her problems weren't really her fault. They were forced on her by her dad and uncle. A dad and uncle who assumed they were invincible and could get away with anything. The anything here being they'd stolen money from their clients. Clients that they had had for years. The same people who came to her graduation parties and she'd gone to their kids' weddings. People she considered family and thought her dad and uncle had too.

For years she'd thought that her dad and uncle's financial firm was one of a kind. A true 'for the people' firm. And then last year, her world fell apart. The firm was accused of funneling funds from clients. But the kicker, at least for Leah, was that it was her mom's best friend Charlotte who'd made the allegations.

Charlotte's husband, Brad had passed away and Charlotte took over the family finances. When she found some discrepancies, she'd gone right to Leah's dad. After months of her dad putting her off, Charlotte felt she had no option but to go to the authorities. Before she did that though, she confronted Leah's mom and asked if she knew anything about it.

Leah's mom had been dumbfounded and told her friend to do what she felt she had to do. And that was basically how both Leah and her mom, Helen, had ended up testifying against her dad and uncle.

They had both been blind to the things that were going on and as much as Leah had thought she had loved her dad unconditionally, there was no way she could sit by and let innocent people lose all their money.

They both felt that they hadn't known enough to help convict them, but it turns out they unwittingly knew enough.

So now her dad and uncle were in prison for a minimum of fifteen years and her mom was a basket case who couldn't figure out a way to live without money. She was used to the finer things in life and now that all the money was gone or frozen, she was forced to work. Perish the thought.

And Leah, well she was sick to death of the press and people thinking that she had to have known what her dad was doing. So sick in fact, that she had been hiding out in her apartment for the last two months.

Until she got the call from her old friend and college roommate. Carly knew how hard this had all been for Leah. And knew that she could use a break. But when Carly asked her to run her new dance studio that she was opening, Leah felt like it would only cause problems.

Carly assured her that no one in Cedarville had probably even heard of her and even if they had, they wouldn't assume that just because her dad was a thief, that she would be too.

Leah still hadn't been sure but then that same day, the company she worked for let her go. They told her it was because of downsizing but she knew the real reason. And as much as she didn't want to cause problems for her friend, she had no choice but to take Carly's offer.

There was no way she would get another job in New York, at least not any job that handled money. And since she was an accountant, that left her out of options.

So here she was, more emotionally exhausted than she could ever remember being, driving down the main street of Cedarville.

All she wanted was a bed and several hours of uninterrupted sleep.

Following her GPS's prompts, she turned down a few side streets until she stopped her car in front of a big brick house.

This would be her home for the foreseeable future.

The house actually belonged to Carly's childhood friend, Melanie and the two lived there together. Melanie had inherited the house from her grandparents and both she and Carly moved into it together after college. When Carly offered Leah a job she also offered her a rent free place to live which made it even harder to say no to her old friend.

Grabbing her phone and her handbag, Leah opened the car door and stepped out into the warm Spring air. It was only the end of April, but the weather was unseasonably warm. Taking only a small backpack that held her essentials from the back seat, Leah made her way to the front door.

Carly had said that neither she or Melanie would be there when she got in but there was a key under the mat on the porch.

Stepping up onto the porch, she was just bending down to check the mat when the porch light came on and the front door opened.

Straightening with the assumption that it was Carly, Leah came face-to-face – or chest as it would be – with a man. A very chiseled man.

"Stop right there," his deep voice bellowed.

When she finally looked up at his face, she got the distinct feeling that he didn't know she was supposed to be there.

"Who are you and what are you doing on my property?"

A couple years ago, she wouldn't have hesitated to bust his balls or maybe do other things with his balls. Not that she knew that many things to do with balls. But ever since the court case, she'd lost her mojo, both in everyday life and sexually. So doing anything with his balls was not in the cards in this moment.

"Isn't this twenty-seven Shadow Lane?" she asked quietly.

His brow furrowed. "It is. Who are you?" He seemed to let his guard down, but only a little.

"I'm Leah and I'm going to be living here with Carly and Melanie."

He stared at her for a beat before saying, "Wait right here," and then shutting the door in her face.

"What the hell?" she said out loud. He just shut the damn door in her face. She'd just driven nine frickin hours to have the door slammed in her face. And yeah, technically he didn't slam the door, but that was not the point.

Without even thinking she pounded her fist on the door. "Hey!" she shouted. The door flew open and there was chiseled chest with a phone to his ear.

"She's right here, hold on." He handed her the phone that had previously been pressed to his ear.

When she just stared at it he said, "It's Carly."

Taking the phone from him she turned so she didn't have to face him. "Hello."

"Leah," she heard Carly's voice. "I'm so sorry that I forgot to mention to my cousin Brandon that you'd be coming. He volunteered to come by and stay with my dog since Melanie and I stayed at the studio to work all night."

"It's fine," Leah said. So chiseled chest had a name and he was Carly's cousin.

"Ignore his attitude," Carly said. "He's angry by nature."

She turned back to face him, phone still to her ear. He appeared to be more relaxed. "I don't plan on having a deep conversation with him. I just drove all night to get here and all I want to do is fall into bed."

"He'll point you in the right direction and I will see you tomorrow."

They said their goodnights and Leah held out the phone for Carly's cousin without saying anything.

"I'm sorry for thinking you were trespassing," Brandon said. "I had no idea you were coming."

She shrugged. "I'm sure I would have done the same thing." She was getting more tired by the second and her body felt like it was going to give out very soon.

"Why don't I show you to your room," he said and stood aside for her to enter the house.

It was dark inside and she couldn't really make out what the room looked like. They were both silent as she followed him through what she assumed was the living room and then up the stairs.

"This is your room," he said and pointed to a door on the left. She started to walk in and then her ingrained manners got the better of her.

"Thank you. I'm sure it was strange for you to find a random person on the porch at three in the morning."

His lips curved into a sly smile and for the second time that night, she felt off balance. "It wasn't so bad. Good night, Leah."

She wanted to watch him walk away but her head was swimming from exhaustion and heat. And not the kind of heat you get from Ohio in April. The kind that stems from a half naked man smiling at you.

Maybe moving to Cedarville hadn't been such a bad idea after all.

By the time she woke up, it was well after ten. At first, she couldn't believe that she'd slept so long, but considering that she hadn't had more than three hours of sleep in a row since the trial had started, she wasn't surprised.

Not sure if Carly and Melanie were home yet, she quickly changed and made her way to find the bathroom.

The house was quiet when she opened her bedroom door and she didn't hear any noise. She found the bathroom right across the hall and made quick work of peeing and brushing her teeth.

Heading downstairs, she still heard nothing. But sitting on the kitchen counter next to a pot of hot coffee she found a note.

Leah,

I've left for the day and to my knowledge Carly and Melanie should be back this morning.

Brandon.

Oh and Max, Carly's dog is outside.

Blunt and to the point Carly thought.

Pouring herself a cup of coffee in a mug that was sitting on the counter, she contemplated the note. He wasn't chatty, that was for sure. But could she blame him? It's not like they knew each other. Sure he'd smiled at her and she'd practically melted on the spot, but that was her issue. Not his. And that probably only happened because she hadn't had sex in fucking forever.

God she missed sex.

Hot, sweaty, curl your toes sex.

And yeah, technically she'd never had that kind of sex before, but a girl could dream.

So really she missed, boring, missionary, roll over and leave when you're done sex.

And that was just sad. Sad that at twenty-eight there had been no passion in her life.

But she was going to change that. Not only was she starting over with a new job and a new place to live, but she was also determined to get back to a better version of who she had been before her world had been turned upside down.

She wanted to go big or go home.

Or at least in theory because this was her home now and she had nowhere else to go and no money to even get there if she did.

Taking her coffee out to the front porch, she saw a dog lounging at the bottom of the steps.

"You must be, Max?" she said and he lifted his head and looked up at her but didn't get up to come greet her.

"My kind of dog," she said and sat down on the swing that was there.

She sipped her coffee enjoying the cool morning and the breeze she was sure came from the lake, when she heard a car pulling up.

When the car stopped, Carly jumped out.

"I can't believe you made it!" She ran up the rest of the drive, stepped over Max and threw her arms around Leah for a hug.

Carly had always been a hugger. Even on the first day of college when they'd just met, she hugged Leah like six times.

"Hey Carls," Leah said and hugged her back. It felt so good to have a friend who didn't care at all that her family was a bunch of criminals.

"You don't know how excited I am," Carly said, stepping back to take her in. "You need to eat."

Leah was aware that she'd lost weight during the trial and she hated it because it made her look frail. "I know, I'm working on it."

"How was the drive?" Carly asked and they both sat down on the swing.

"Uneventful. At least until I got here."

"I really am sorry about Brandon. By the time you told me you were coming, Mel and I already had plans to paint the studio and I had forgotten I'd asked Brandon to come stay with Max."

She waved her hand. "It was fine. I just took him by surprise."

"He can be a pain-in-the-ass sometimes but he means well."

"He made coffee this morning, so pain-in-the-ass or not, I'm grateful to him."

Carly laughed. "Let's go inside so I can get myself some of that coffee."

Leah refilled her own cup after Carly filled her mug.

"How are you doing really?" Carly asked.

Leah sighed. "Honestly? Pretty shitty."

"I can't even imagine what you are going through."

"Wanna know the worst part?" Leah asked her friend. "It's that I'm afraid to do or say anything that isn't completely proper or normal. Which means all day, I have to think everything I say through. Everything. Even to cashiers in stores. Because if I say one thing that could be misconstrued, I'm screwed."

"You won't have to worry about that here. No one is going to know who you are, especially now that you're using your mom's last name."

Leah had decided, even before she'd chosen to move to Cedarville, that instead of being Leah Gibson, she was going to use her mom's maiden name and go by Leah Britton. That way even if people thought they recognized her face, they wouldn't know the name.

"I hope you're right because I'm ready to be myself again."

"You'll get there," Carly said.

"So tell me more about the dance studio?"

"It's going to be so amazing, Leah! I can't wait for you to see the space we're renting. It's ten thousand square feet and we are going to have four separate studios. Right now it is just me and Mel teaching but we wanted more space in case we grow."

"That's good planning. When do you open?"

"We," Carly said. "We open in two weeks."

She knew her friend was trying to include her in the business but she wasn't an owner. Just the manager.

"It's your business, Carly, I'm just working there."

"Fuck that, Leah." Carly always loved to use the f-word. She swore up and down that dancers had the worst potty mouths. "You may not be giving us any money but I plan on working you like a dog. I am shit with books and management and so is Mel. All we have to do is teach, you have to do everything else. So yes, we...are a 'we' and don't you forget it."

Leah wanted to cry at how nice her friend was being. But on her car ride to Cedarville she made a promise to herself that she was not going to cry anymore. She had done enough crying for a lifetime and she was done with it.

Happy was her new go-to emotion and she planned on using every tool in her arsenal to get there everyday.

Lightning Source UK Ltd.
Milton Keynes UK
UKHW011328081222
413590UK00001B/341